Doctor Darw

Waterloo

Pigeon

A Novel of 19th Century Shrewsbury

By
Henry Andrew Quinn

Dr Darwin's Waterloo Pigeon
by
Henry Andrew Quinn
drdarwin@hotmail.co.uk

ISBN: 1481855026

Published by Henry Andrew Quinn in conjunction with Writersworld Ltd

Edited by James Quinn and Brian Stanton

Cover designed by Jag Lall

Printed and bound by
www.printondemand-worldwide.com

www.writersworld.co.uk
Writersworld, 2 Bear Close Flats, Bear Close,
Woodstock, Oxfordshire, OX20 1JX, United Kingdom

**The text pages of this book are produced via an independent certification
process than ensures the trees from which the paper is produced come from
well managed sources that exclude the risk of using illegally logged
timber while leaving options to use recycled paper as well.**

Disclaimer

All stories herein are a work of fiction. The characters do not exist, except in the mind of the author. Any resemblance to persons, living or dead, is purely coincidental. Mr Henry Andrew Quinn accepts no personal or legal liability or responsibility for the accuracy, completeness, or references within this fictional work.

Acknowledgements

The author would like to thank the history of Shrewsbury and its buildings, the diaries of Anne Barbour and the wonderful local studies library in Shrewsbury for the immense inspiration they provide. The author would also like to extend his gratitude to Neil Sambrook.

To my wife Liz - All my love forever and a day.

To my son James.

Contents

Author's Note -
Shrewsbury in the 19th Century

The following is a story of the times surrounding the Napoleonic War. From 1797 until 1815 war raged throughout Europe until its climax and Napoleon's ultimate defeat at the Battle of Waterloo. The insurmountable financial pressure of the war left the British economy in dire straits and as a direct resolution to the strain an income tax was introduced nearing the end of the 18th Century to offset the cost of the vital weapons and supplies necessary to equip the fighting forces. The consequential tax was to be levied at a previously unseen ten percent against every income over £200 a year. It was later estimated that the overall cost to Britain for fighting the Napoleonic Wars was ultimately in excess of 30 million pounds, equivalent to more than 1 billion pounds today.

This is the tale of the people involved in the secretive business of moving money around Europe in the days when cash was king and huge fortunes were being made by fair or foul means. Men of wealth were constantly seeking ways to hide their illicit earnings but were constantly mindful that financial gain to the detriment of the country was treason, which in times of war meant only one thing, an appointment at the gallows with a duly earned death sentence.

In these antiquated times the town of Shrewsbury, with its population of only 14,000, was the metropolis of a considerable rural area. The poorly kept roads and primitive transport of the time made the City of London almost as remote as Paris or Rome. Encircled by the River Severn and a thriving town in its own right, Shrewsbury contained a wealthy aristocracy and comfortable middle-class. For the most part of the year these wealthy interlopers would inhabit the country houses and estates of the luscious Welsh border only ever thinking of Shrewsbury as their meeting-place and winter residence. The wealthy often took town houses during the months when many of the country paths and lanes were passable only on horseback. Theirs was a segment of society that endlessly prospered, particularly during the war years, when rising corn-prices produced higher rents and corresponding profits.

The town, as it remains to this day, was almost entirely situated within the main loop of the deep swift-flowing Severn and confined within the limits of its great medieval Castle walls. Over the years, these walls had been reduced in height and stripped of their battlements and towers but many scenic walks could be taken from the remnants of the boundary walls to the outskirts of Shrewsbury Town. At the neck of the Severn's loop stood the old red stone Castle, crumbling yet picturesque, looking down from its elevation over the many houses and poorly paved cobbled streets. Many of the larger timbered houses dated from the sixteenth century but between their overhanging casement frontages appeared newer and more fashionable constructions with pillared facades. These were built alongside tumbledown cottages of thatch and plaster and shops with small dark windows. Improvements were imperative and early in the new century people became increasingly agitated, seeking "better paving, lighting, cleaning, watering and regulating." Calls to improve access to the town had not gone unheard and in 1792 work began on the Welsh Bridge that crossed the Severn to Frankwell, with the bridge finally opened in 1795. The campaign to widen streets and bring improvements to the town's squares was an extension and continuation of the bridge project.

Shrewsbury society was inevitably snobbish, bigoted and renowned for its exclusivity. For members of this elite group there was a near-continuous round of balls, suppers, oyster-feasts and six o'clock dinner-parties. Hunting was provided for the more active sportsmen and for the less strenuously inclined, strolling players often entertained in the assembly hall. Speakers and preachers were also regular visitors to the town. Hostesses constantly strove to raise the standard of hospitality and as a result each social gathering became a little more lavish than the last. On such occasions chatter was infectious and gossip rife.

During the closing decade of the eighteenth century, London became closer as improvements to roads and faster coach services made the capital far more accessible. Shortly afterwards the burgeoning national railway system embraced the town and its days of isolation were over. Hindsight has judged this event as the last blossoming of the flower that was Shrewsbury, which Daniel Defoe had once described using the following words: *"It was a fine place to live, a large, pleasant, populous and rich town; full of gentry and yet full of trade too.* **"**

Waterloo Pigeon

ONE

THE FUNERAL

During the twenty-five years it had conducted burials, the churchyard of the new St Chad's Church, close to Shrewsbury town centre, had rarely seen a more sombre event quite like the one that unfolded on the morning of Saturday 23rd August 1817. The military colours of every local regiment were on display in all their sharpness and finery, providing a vivid backdrop for the large mournful crowd who filed to the graveside. As the funeral service inside the church itself had lasted almost two hours many among the gathering were glad to finally step outside from the clammy confines of the crowded aisles. But their relief at finally being able to gasp at some fresh air soon evaporated, shuffling as they did out onto the ground that lay burnt from the power of a high midday sun.

There was not a single breath of breeze to disturb the leaves on the tall trees overlooking the graveyard that day, but amongst the gathered mourners a frigid air of great sadness prevailed. The awkward chill was valiantly offsetting the blistering late-summer heat that threatened to consume them all. Nobody was spared the discomfort, caused not only by the icy grief but also by the soaring temperatures. Standing out in front of the distinguished assembly even the Mayor of Shrewsbury, the right honourable Joshua Peele, a man of considerable girth and as Dr Darwin often said, "That is the sort of nose that you do not get going to bed with a glass of milk at eight o' clock." To put it bluntly he liked a drop and Peele was suffering from this curious mixture of warmth and chill. Nevertheless it was his own well-intentioned, if overlong oration about the deceased that had kept the congregation far too long in the church.

Outwardly glowing due to sunburn and perspiration, an inner radiance slowly returned to Peele as he began looking at those around him. Such unusually hot weather made drinking a necessity so there was no better time to be the most successful wine merchant in the area. There was little doubt in his lucrative mind that significant amounts would be imbibed at the great feast, due to take place shortly at the nearby Lion Hotel. Of course Peele, who was a Freeman of the Borough, had supplied it all. He too joined the family of the deceased at the graveside. Together with fellow officers from the dead soldier's regiment, the funeral's attendees guaranteed an unrivalled turn out and Peele's spirits soared at the thought of the impending consumption. Among their number was local born General Rowland Hill, a war hero from the Battle of Waterloo only two years previous, when the significantly outnumbered British troops rallied to defeat Napoleon's army and succeeded to redraw the map of Europe. It was Hill who had ensured the British forces were in a position to drive Napoleon's infamous old guard from the field and ultimately secure victory.

From a lookout, merely yards away from the church grounds and safely hidden from onlookers by the evergreen trees all around, an inquisitive young boy looked over this congregation with a fine mix of wonderment and curiosity. All the while he methodically scrutinized through the open schoolroom window and searched for the reason why such a large and conspicuous crowd should be present at the funeral of a solider he knew to be of only modest rank. Indeed, the observation powers of this particular boy would go down in history and so it is hardly surprising that Charles Darwin would remember what he saw on this Saturday morning for the rest of his long and pioneering life. As his dear Mother had died only a month previous, funeral services were still raw in his mind, however Charles would later recall what he saw unfolding before him with a clarity that escaped him when recollecting the day his dear Mother was laid to rest.

For the past two years Charles had known the deceased as a patient of his father, the inimitable Doctor Robert Darwin. Together they had often visited this very sick man whose wounds required constant treatment and dressing. The Doctor had constantly assured Charles that this enterprising solider had been a hero of Waterloo. It was therefore something of a mystery to Charles that his father, who had regularly sang the praises of this battle-scarred veteran, was nowhere to be seen amongst those gathered by the graveside or anywhere else in view.

There was little or no time to ruminate on Dr. Darwin's whereabouts as the ceremony moved on apace and the burial party was soon joined by a horse with full military saddle, boots placed wrong way about in the stirrups and carbine in its holster. Charles was confused rather than impressed as this solider had never been an officer and as he took note of the occasion he silently queried the need for such pageantry. Following the days of the great battle at Waterloo, funerals of this nature had become familiar to him as well as many other schoolboys in the land where numerous fine young men had succumbed to their war-bound injuries.

The rider-less horse was led to the graveside where the attendees standing solemnly in the sunlight listened to the funeral dirge of Reverend Jefferson.

"William Matthews", he began, turning his head to address those standing behind him, "a native of Frankwell, Shrewsbury and late of the Fifteenth Hussars, whom we have brought to this place to bury and rest in the arms of the Lord."

The Reverend paused for a moment as another turn of his head caused him to blink when bright sunlight brushed across his face. He continued, "Many fine words have been spoken this glorious morning of the brave deeds performed against the French cavalry in the English squares and in the Hougoumont Chateau, by Matthews at the field of Waterloo. I feel there is little to be added to them by me, except to remember the text of Joshua 24:30: *"And they buried him in the land of his inheritance."*

Although it may have escaped the Reverend's notice a look of self-satisfaction was evident on the faces of a number of Shrewsbury's Freeman and business fraternity present that day. Both the local banker Mr Rocke, a tall man with a large beard, dressed immaculately in frock coat and sporting a dapper wig with a tail (which he thought gave him a look of importance much like a barrister in High Court) and his friend Mr Loxdale, a local man who was a blind partner in Rocke's Bank were passing especially coy smiles. The quick mindful glances that passed between them, however, did not escape the attention of young Charles Darwin who watched on from his high vigil. At that very moment the morning air echoed with the sound of gunfire as the small guard of honour released a volley of shots into the sky in honour of their fallen colleague. Although startled by the blasts, Charles felt nothing but pride and looked on respectfully as the coffin was lowered silently into the ground. He refrained from making any gesture to save drawing attention to himself and was content enough to watch as the multitude of mourners tossed flowers into the open grave as they passed by.

Throughout the morning Charles had paid his undivided attention to the activity in the churchyard, in turn causing a neglect of the schoolwork set by Reverend Augustus Case, his teacher and also the Vicar of Shrewsbury's Unitarian Church. It was there that he had worshipped with his Mother on Sunday mornings, until just before her death. The Reverend Case was a tall, angular man with sunken blue eyes, whose clothes hung loosely from his slender frame. In the strict, but gentle tone often used by the Reverend when teaching, he asked Charles to "return to the task before him," pointing at the book that was closed and pushed to the side of the desk where Charles sat. Many times Charles had heard his father state that Reverend Case only remained at the school and indeed the Unitarian Church, at the insistence of Charles' mother, Susannah Darwin. Herself being the eldest daughter of Josiah Wedgwood who was known as 'The Great Potter of England.' Acting upon his teacher's instruction he re-opened the book but as he did he shot one last glance out of the window, a glance that was prolonged by finally catching sight of his much beloved father, Doctor Robert Darwin.

Known locally as 'the Father of Frankwell' he was the most instantly recognisable man in Shrewsbury, not least due to his rotund, ample figure. His dress at this period was invariably a snuff-coloured cloth suit, coat, waistcoat and gaiters of the same shade buttoned above the knees; his waistcoat had the old fashioned lappet above the pockets with wide cuffs to his coat. His shirt-frill and tightly folded necktie were expensive but understated. Aside from the heavy, conspicuous watch-chain there were was no other cosmetic finery attached to this plain unpretentious gentleman. He was a Whig by upbringing and inclination, vehemently anti-Tory and critical of aristocrats whose fortunes were rooted in hereditary privilege. He had a remarkable head for business and local folklore had it that: *"Two thirds of Shrewsbury owed him money and he knew the medical secrets of the other third."*

Given his importance and standing in the community Charles found it strange that his father should stand toward the rear of a group of such local luminaries, yet the look on the Doctor's face made him one of them. Mr Rocke had worn almost the same expression only moments before. That such silent exchanges of communication were evident on today of all days gave Charles something else to ponder, but there was no time to dwell on such matters as Reverend Case turned around at the front of the class and shot Charles a puzzled glance of his own. With the undue aplomb of a scolded schoolboy, Charles hurriedly opened the book before him and began to study once again.

TWO

CURIOSITY AROUSED

Doctor Darwin stood in front of the great pillars of St. Chad's Church and looked out over the glorious parkland known to Shrewsbury as the Quarry. The morning sunshine blazed in such a manner that the landscape before the Doctor absorbed his concentration completely, while also managing to cast his vast shadow far behind him. Standing six feet five inches tall and weighing over 300 pounds, the Doctor himself was a mighty structure. Despite his colossal build he was an energetic man, although sometimes prone to bouts of fatigue and with the temperature soaring he had already begun to feel considerably weary. It was well known in Shrewsbury that due to his remarkable frame he never came downstairs forwards; always backwards just in case he should topple over. On entering an old timber framed house (and heaven knows Shrewsbury had more than its share) he would always get his coachman to test the stairs and if they were not sufficiently safe to take his weight, the coachman would carry on up in order to shout down the symptoms of the patient. Shifting his gaze from the idyllic summer views of the Quarry and the ever-sluicing Severn, the Doctor looked upward toward the Church's pillars and his thoughts wandered back to religious matters.

More agnostic than atheist, he had always found himself ambivalent towards religion. The good Doctor could simply not understand why it was such a sin to presume that God would always help those who call for Him but also a sin to be despondent of God when that help failed to arrive. He had given much thought to the biblical notion of the earth being merely 4,500 years old and how this contradicted the notions of a local man of the church, namely Reverend Blakeway, an apparent authority on such matters. Blakeway estimated that one boulder he had examined in Shrewsbury had existed for at least two million years, a stark and worrying query, in the face of the Church's authority. The Doctor quickly altered the course of his thoughts as these were not matters worthy of lengthy contemplation on such a morning as this and he continued moving in a leisurely if somewhat painstaking fashion toward his oncoming carriage. As he had made not even ten paces into his journey an instantly recognisable voice brought the doctor to a halt.

"Well, well, what could the great Doctor Darwin of Shrewsbury possibly be doing at a military funeral?"

The familiar voice belonged to Catherine Plymley, a local lady in her mid-fifties, whose unmarried and childless past gave the impression of a woman somewhat younger. Her attractive features and skin of fine china were of no great consequence to Doctor Darwin, but her question did give rise to some disquiet within him as she was renowned as a keen diarist, in addition to being Shrewsbury town's keenest rumourmonger.

"Men in need of a doctor, my dear Miss Plymley," he answered, "do not define their placing in life. This is just a former patient, alas who no longer needs any assistance from me."

Inwardly impressed by his own response, Doctor Darwin sought to move the conversation away from matters of conscience to matters of the day: "And how are you this fine if unhappy morning?"

Miss Plymley was not prepared to let small talk thwart her enquiries. "My dear Doctor, the thought of you, a man of peace, involved with a hero of Waterloo arouses my curiosity." There was no disguising the irritation in Doctor Darwin's reply.

"Whatever do you mean by 'involved'... Hmm?" The Doctor paused for a moment but with his carriage quickly approaching, he continued to be as evasive as possible. "Miss Plymley, I am afraid that there is nothing of interest to you on this sad occasion, merely a funeral for an acquaintance. Madam I must bid you good morning." With that Doctor Darwin moved abruptly toward his carriage. Glancing back to where the lady stood, he avoided catching her gaze, as the words of Jonathan Swift ran through his mind, for the Irish poet did not speak kindly of gossips.

> *Nor do they trust their tongue alone,*
> *but speak a language of their own,*
> *Can read a nod, a shrug, a look,*
> *far better than a printed book,*
> *Convey a libel with a frown,*

and wink a reputation down.

There was no doubt in anyone's mind that Catherine Plymley was the biggest scandalmonger in Shrewsbury. The Doctor was well aware of her infamous diaries containing gossip and news of Shrewsbury and its inhabitants. While always mindful of never inviting her to his dinner table, she was never short of invitations due in no small measure to the position of high office held in Government by her brother. The thought of her insinuation and wagging tongue made him think of a piece of advice he often gave himself: "Never pick a quarrel with those that buy their ink in gallons."

The Doctor climbed into the carriage but had travelled no more than a few dozen yards when he called out to his thickset coach driver Mark, who also served as his protector from the disorderly. "Mark, on such a lovely morning I think I shall actually walk the remainder. So, carry on and take the coach back to the Mount. Inform my daughter Marianne that I have no appointments today and will just take an idle stroll back home."

The Doctor went the long way around the Quarry in order to avoid any further inquisitions from Miss Plymley. This path took him along St Chad's Terrace where he turned into Quarry Place, encountering the round cobblestones that formed the paving known locally as "petrified kidneys." This was a form of paving detested by his father-in-law Josiah Wedgwood, who would often manage to break his wooden 'peg' leg on such stones when visiting Shrewsbury, ensuring another costly order to the manufacturers in Portsmouth. The sight of a large timbered-framed house prompted his memory to wander back to his early days in Shrewsbury and he began to think of the day he arrived at the very house that now stood before him, the home of William Tayluer, a surgeon and family friend of the Wedgwood family.

On that day in November 1786 his worldly wealth was £20; One pound for every year of his life and given to him by his father Erasmus Darwin. He came to Shrewsbury with a recommendation from his father to William Tayluer that his son be made a partner in the medical practice owned by the surgeon. Doctor Darwin had come fresh from Edinburgh "the Athens of The North." He studied first at the great medical school of Leyden, a highly acclaimed establishment that guaranteed qualified doctors who were guaranteed to be far advanced in their medical knowledge than any contemporary Shrewsbury doctor could ever dream. Within six months he had established a practice of between forty and fifty patients and soon it was said around the town that there no longer remained a need to send to the nearest city, Birmingham, for doctors. Doctor Darwin had bought a run down property in the St John's Hill part of Shrewsbury and after buying more properties in the area he began increasing rents, much to the disgust of his tenants. To the Doctor this was business, an avenue where sentiment had no place.

This shrewd understanding of money was to serve Doctor Darwin well as, since the war there had been a growing mistrust of banks which were prone to failure and in a town such as Shrewsbury most of the wealthy had land and property but not cash. Doctor Darwin was quick to realise that there was a significant need for an efficient arrangement of mortgages relating to these properties, particularly given that at the time they were greatly under-valued and ripe for investment. Where the health of a patient was concerned the Doctor was capable of great compassion befitting a medical man, but in business he was ruthless often using methods that were unsavoury to say the least. One did not default on a loan to Doctor Darwin. To do so would have been at great personal risk.

The loans were based on lenders paying back less in the early years when their business venture was growing but more when it matured. They paid extra in rates for this privilege. One secret of his success stemmed from his wealthy clients' wives, who would come to him with some trivial excuse of ill health which the doctor quickly diagnosed. He would then say: "Come now, what's the real reason for your visit? Is it your husband not showing you affection and being unkind and uncaring?"

They would take this opportunity to unravel their woes at which point Doctor Darwin would quickly explain the root of her husband's inconsiderate treatment was 'money'. He would then proceed to tell them about his mortgages and money lending schemes, recommending to the patient she return home and show great knowledge of finance and thus the means to solve their problems. This ploy rarely failed and within mere days of the Doctor's recommendations their husbands would arrive to borrow money, whilst also bringing the kind regards of his wife "who felt much better now, thank you." The Doctor steadied himself against a low-slung yet finely carved wall surveying the river before him. When without warning his eyes began to fill with tears at the thought of his own dear wife Susannah, who so recently had gone to her lonesome grave. The first and only love of his life, she had been the eldest daughter of Josiah Wedgwood. The Doctor recalled her illness futilely; knowing now that a blockage and subsequent leaking into the body had fatally poisoned her. He knew it was possible to put people into some kind of deep sleep where they felt nothing of pain until a doctor had operated. It was a simple operation that he felt sure one day would be carried out but his dislike of blood and mistrust of self-proclaimed surgeons left him very cold. The responsibility lay heavily on his mind but he also knew his wife would never have withstood the trauma of such an invasive operation.

She died leaving him and their six children with a constant income and large sum of inheritance. Most of the funds were available in cash from the huge Wedgwood fortune of which Susannah had been entitled to a quarter. It amounted to a mammoth sum, with the Wedgwood pottery business in a very healthy state as her father Josiah rarely gave credit, demanding all arrears paid in due course. The Doctor felt his wife's declining health had been due to her frequent maternal condition as she had bore Darwin six children, each one causing a further strain on her physical well being. He solemnly blamed her early demise as a consequence of half a dozen difficult pregnancies.

Walking on past the great timber framed house of Doctor Tayluer and into the Quarry park, Darwin stopped momentarily to observe on his right, the Dingle, the Quarry's park within a park. Like an island in the middle of the Quarry's ocean the Dingle was a fenced off and hedge-rowed dip into the smooth landscape containing a miniature set of ponds and heavily flowered walkways. In the pool of the Dingle his youngest son Charles spent school breaks from his nearby classroom catching newts to take home and dissect on the kitchen table until Anne, the cook, complained to the Doctor who was forced to tell young Charles to stop. With the overcrowding and shortage of space in Shrewsbury, the Quarry was a Godsend to the townsfolk; this beautiful green-pastured open space gave people a location to roam freely or even graze cattle. The fenced off land in the centre of the Quarry had also become infamous over the years as a place of public executions. Many times over the Reverend John Brickdale-Blakeway, Shrewsbury's foremost historian, had told how a woman was burnt at the stake in the Dingle. The Quarry had also been used on occasions of rejoicing such as the recent return of one of the great "lions" of the period, Lord Hill, a local born hero. When he returned from the Peninsular War in 1814, so great was the crowd and so eager were they to welcome him, Hill was almost crushed to death. If he had died in Shrewsbury that day thought the Doctor, the lives of certain others would be far different today.

As Doctor Darwin carried on past the Dingle and carried on down the incline towards the banks of the Severn, he stopped, wiped his brow and felt himself gripped by thirst. He knew refreshment could be found just across the Severn and simply by boarding the little ferry he would be taken to the Prince of Wales public house on the opposite bank. He made his way down to the riverside and hailed the ferry with the customary cry of "boatman" and watched as the figure of one of his patients, a Mr Tom Shelvock, shuffled to the rivers edge in a tired manner. At first, it crossed his mind that the poor fellow was struggling with the heat but on second thought, it was just as likely Tom had taken to imbibing alcohol once again. Tom climbed aboard the large, rickety, skiff-type boat that was old and showing signs of neglect. Desperately requiring a coat of paint, it was unlike Tom to allow his boat to fall into a state of disrepair, something that did not go unnoticed by the Doctor.

Tom proceeded to haul, by means of a rope stretched across the river, the skiff and himself toward the riverbank on which the Doctor stood. Darwin climbed aboard, his great weight causing the skiff to roll around and as he took his seat received a half-hearted greeting from the boatman who muttered, "A good-day to you and long may you enjoy this day."

The Doctor looked sternly at Tom's jaundiced complexion. For a man of 50 years of age he was in poor health. "Still at the bottle I see," he said referring to Tom's colour and added, "I have told you before Tom, that if you kept on drinking your liver will surely give out on you."

"God knows I do try Doctor but it is mighty hard when all I deal out all day is the bottle" replied Tom meekly, pointing to the Prince of Wales of which he was the proprietor.

"Well," he replied, "it is your life." Doctor Darwin sensed a change of tack was required and quickly added, "But it is far too pleasant a day to spoil on talk of death and illness. I would like a long cool drink with no alcohol please when we reach the Prince."

As Tom took the skiff from one side of the Severn to the other, Doctor Darwin in a jovial tone, asked, "How goes the fishing today Tom? Any luck with the 'The Fish of King Arthur'?" Knowing Tom was sensitive on the subject, the Doctor was given a reply he would have been able to guarantee.

"You may joke Doctor but I did see that fish, it was at least eight to ten feet long! It had a mighty girth and it wore a belt, I swear on it! And on that belt, sir, was the most ornate golden sword encrusted with jewels. I will trawl the entire length of the River Severn if needs be..." Tom paused after his determined speech staring sternly into Dr. Darwin's eyes. "What if, indeed, I am to be the finder of the fabled sword of King Arthur?" Tom continued, while the Doctor became more aware that they had stopped right in the middle of the Severn. The Doctor's brow began to sweat anew. "Somewhere around these parts, it is written that he threw Excalibur into the water but it was a fish, not a lady, which slipped its head through the belt. Some say it was in a pool near Shrewsbury and I tell you Doctor as I have before, I have laid eyes on him on two different occasions right there in the deepest part of the river." Tom turned wildly and pointed to the dark waters.

The Doctor watched Tom with hidden concern and chose not to reply. All the while there was a story going through his mind, once told to him by his historian friend Reverend Blakeway that would have taken the wind right out of poor Tom's sails.

Blakeway had told the Doctor that many years before in a village outside of town there was a great pool which was rumoured to be connected underground to the River Severn. The local squire had a lifelong battle with a giant fish but one day took the upper hand and managed to catch it. With assistance from on-lookers, the squire managed to hoist it into his boat but arguments soon ensued as to how big its girth was. They decided the squire was roughly the same size around his middle so was asked to take off his belt so it could be measured later. After much struggle they fastened the belt onto the fish along with the squire's jewel encrusted sword, which had been presented to him for good work in the county.

Without warning the fish then made an almighty leap, creating an enormous splash as it crashed into the water. It disappeared into the pool wearing the belt and sword and despite the squire's incessant searching he never did retrieve his bejewelled belt. For many years afterward the fish was sighted on various occasions in both the pool and River Severn. Surely by now the Doctor presumed the fish must be of a great age, if still alive at all. Since the story was now all but forgotten by many Salopians poor Tom must be right; he had seen the fabled fish but had simply attached the wrong story to it. Romantically, but in error, he believed it to be the story of King Arthur's Excalibur and how, when the King lay dieing, he sent a servant to throw the sword of solid gold into a great pool near to Shrewsbury. The Doctor held his tongue for want of reaching the other side of the river in a timely manner and sure enough Tom soon abated his rants and delivered the Doctor safely.

As they reached the opposite side, the Doctor, without undue strain, managed the short incline to the old dilapidated house that served as a hostel. He sat down heavily on the wooden bench outside removing his weighty cloth coat for greater comfort. Darwin took a deep breath and then another while he sat waiting for Tom to bring his refreshment. The sun was like a great torch of fire beaming onto his large frame and in trying to relax, took from his waistcoat the gold watch inherited from his mother. "Time stands still on days like this," he thought with the conversation continuing inside his head, "and I have no visits to make this day unless there is an emergency." His coachman Mark would have informed the Darwin's eldest daughter Marianne (who had taken on the daily running of the house since the death of her Mother) by now of her father's intention to spend some time on his own. Tom brought a large glass of lemon juice to the Doctor who consumed it quickly in order to quench his thirst and with the sun easing his eyes closed, began to doze.

The memories of the morning slowly went through his mind. What if that Plymley woman knew the real story of the day's events? They would really set fire to the pages of her infamous diaries.

It all seemed so long ago now since the dinner party at Mount House, given in honour of Sir Rowland Hill (widely known as Daddy Hill for the way he looked after the soldiers of the British Army), the hero of the Peninsular War and recently appointed second in command of the British Army, his only superior being General Wellington no less.

The Doctor had chosen to build the family home, Mount House, on The Mount just outside of the confines of Shrewsbury town, on the Welsh-side of the river. At the time it was a far less fashionable location than the over-priced English side of the River Severn and the site for his home was based across the Welsh Bridge, beyond and above the dilapidated district of Frankwell, an area given its original name Frankville in ancient times by the French who came with the Normans in 1066. His father had an adage of: "Always take your water before a Town, not in or after it." Since the town of Shrewsbury put all its sewerage into the Severn at the Welsh Bridge and took its drinking water further down river at the English Bridge this may well have been a serious point of consideration when Doctor Darwin had chosen this site. Mount House had its critics and was described by one as "an uninspired three storey Georgian house of red brick; square, substantial and ugly." But among its redeeming features was the view from the pristine green lawns at the rear that looked out over the curling Severn below to the rolling pastures and woods beyond. Away to the right the town was barely visible, with lowly Frankwell tucked out of site behind thick shrubs and hedgerows. When Doctor Darwin was asked why he built such a large house he replied: "Had I built a small one nobody would have enquired about me and would not suppose a person of eminence could live in such a one. But now I intend my house to introduce my name and to pay for itself."

Aware that he had the rest of this luxurious summer's day to wend his way back home as and when it suited him, the Doctor thought of his home with a sense of pride and played back the happenings that took place there only a few years previous.

THREE

The Dinner At Mount House
January 1815

Whatever the cost of the salubrious dinner hosted by Doctor Darwin and his wife at Mount House in January 1815, it would in the years ahead be recouped a thousand-fold. The guest list read like a "who's who" of Shrewsbury nobility. From the entrance of the Mount, surrounded by ready and waiting carriages through to the brightly gas-lit hallways, the Mount was the epitome of dining elegance, indeed all guests present felt well and truly spoilt. Garbed in their fine evening attire the dinner-guests milled from room to hallway and back to the lounge area, their conversations combining to a social furore of overwhelming frivolity. All the while Doctor Darwin presided over the partygoers: constantly making his presence known as he walked among his guests by his kind acknowledgements and comments, as if his gait and height were not enough. All the while on his mingling route he steadily gripped his glass of Port before him but not once did it touch his lips.

The candle and gas light mixed well with the uplifting atmosphere in the Mount House and the Doctor truly began to enjoy his evening.

Two of the last guests to arrive that evening were the particular focus of the Doctor's attention. One was Sir Rowland Hill and the other was an odd-looking bespectacled man with round face, prominent blue eyes and an astute humorous expression. This man was small in stature although not in girth and was named Nathan

Rothschild. Introduced to the Doctor as a merchant banker he had been charged with the task of borrowing and then supplying Wellington's army with gold and silver enabling the Duke to pay his troops. Doctor Darwin had first met this orthodox Jew when he was a merchant in Manchester. However, it was not as a trader that Darwin knew Nathan Rothschild; it was through his money lending business. Initially Doctor Darwin had noticed how ill at ease Nathan Rothschild appeared, although both he and Hill had accepted an invitation to stay the night. Once again there was cunning attached to the Doctor's forward planning as he intended to question them both whilst under the influence of alcohol and within the Doctor's over-bearing hospitality.

Edward Evans, the long-serving manservant of the Darwin family, appeared at the opening of the solarium. Dressed in his black and ageing long-tailed coat, which extended over black breeches and white stockings, he announced in a formal and business-like manner that dinner was to be served. Behind the scenes, preparing their dishes was Anne, the cook; she was an enormous lady who dominated the whole household. Her portly weight was no problem to the Doctor however, as he would often be heard to say many times over, "Never trust a skinny cook."

As a first course she had made ham hocks from a recipe obtained from Sir Rowland's own army cook who was presently consuming a great deal of beer in the kitchen, while telling all the servants how he beat the French in Portugal and Spain, and passing a roving eye in the direction of Anne.

For many years a recurring talking point at the Doctor's dinner table were the words written around the rim of his dinner plates: "Masticate, denticate, chump and chew, then swallow." The Doctor always recommended that food be chewed at least twenty times, while the dinner service of course was Wedgwood supplied from the factory of his late Father in Law at Etruia.

The Doctor's most favourite main course was goose pie, the smell of which had lingered throughout the house for most of the day in question. Goose pie was a renowned delicacy of Shrewsbury, one which was sent all round the midlands, and as coach travel became a lot faster it even made it as far as London. He was insistent on how this dish should be prepared and knew every stage of the process. Flour was required to make the walls of a goose pie which was then layered with a pickled dried tongue and boiled until it was tender enough to peel with the root removed. The next stage involved boning a goose and a large fowl; taking half a quarter ounce of mace to be finely beaten, adding a large teaspoonful of ground pepper, three teaspoonfuls of salt, all added to a pint of stock made from the innards of the poultry, mixing all together and seasoning the fowl and goose with it. Then the fowl is placed in the goose, the tongue in the fowl and the goose in the same manner as if whole. Half a pound of butter is placed on top, in the biggest saucepan available, and then cooked slowly for four hours.

After being ushered through, the guests sat at the great long mahogany table situated in the dining room of Mount House, whose windows offered a panoramic view of the snow-covered countryside. On a large three-faced Welsh dresser were shelves stacked with miniature busts of famous people. Doctor Darwin had taken these as payment for any accountancy work he had carried out on behalf of the Wedgwood Company. The exalted company of persons about to dine were all connected by one defining thread: a common interest in the Old Bank of Shrewsbury. Among those present were John Rocke, Joshua Peele, John Loxdale and always in attendance at the Doctor's social functions to keep conversation at a high standard were the Headmaster of Shrewsbury School, Samuel Butler and the delightfully mannered historian Reverend Brickdale-Blakeway. These two men, along with the Doctor, were collectively known as the 'Shrewsbury Encyclopaedias' for their combined knowledge. All were accompanied by their wives who were being personally taken care of by the Doctor's wife Susannah, who regaled them with stories of London and the social occasions she had witnessed during her stay in the great capital. When she first arrived in Shrewsbury, Susannah had sometimes given the impression of being aloof and overheard such remarks as "Who does she think she is with her airs and graces?…just because she is the daughter of Joshua Wedgwood." But she soon won over any detractors with her knowledge of etiquette, table manners and fashion, and all the while her dinner parties fast became the talk of Shrewsbury.

Last to be seated, but certainly not least in terms of importance was Thomas Eyton, head of the Old Bank of Shrewsbury and also Receiver General of Taxes for Shropshire. Of all the guests that night, it was his integrity that the Doctor most doubted. The senior partner in the Shrewsbury Bank, he was renowned for his pomp and authority, which had led to his ironic nickname 'King Eyton' in and about the town. He was also the Grand Worshipful Master of the Lodge in Shrewsbury that counted Doctor Darwin among its numerous members. Eyton had a reputation for being outspoken and insensitive, with critical remarks never far from his lips. His position and wealth bought him a degree of tolerance but when he made a disparaging remark in a raised voice to the wife of Mr Rocke, his partner at the bank, saying, "Ma'am, those gloves I think have been seen before in Shrewsbury," Susannah Darwin scolded Eyton for his rudeness. Nathan Rothschild was unaware of Eyton's pomposity although his grasp of such social connotations was not thoroughly sufficient to fully comprehend what had truly been said.

With the unknown incident now passed the diners carried on their meal with much aplomb. After the starters had been cleared and the goose pie had just begun to be consumed the Doctor took the chance to interrupt the chitchat with a fond re-telling of his favourite story of Shrewsbury Town's yesteryear. The detail with which the Doctor told this particular tale gave him more than a slight advantage over the Reverend Blakeway. Despite teaching the Doctor a good part of all he knew of the town's past; the Reverend was still unaware of the part the good Doctor played behind the scenes of this particular episode from Shrewsbury's recent past. In the story Doctor Darwin always excluded the full extent of his financial involvement, depending upon the company of course.

Customarily the Doctor lifted his dessert fork and rang it against his glass to draw his guests' attention. As they fell silent, he remained seated (his head height still superior to anyone else at the table) and without further ado, began to tell them his oft-rehearsed and never-bettered dinner story:

Of the unusual occurrences that had taken place in Shrewsbury down the years none was more unfathomable than the fall of the old St Chad's church. This church had dominated the centre of Shrewsbury for over 600 years and the night it collapsed felt like the end of the world for inhabitants of the town. It came to grief in July 1788, the very same month of Doctor Darwin's own arrival to Shrewsbury town. In the small hours of a Sunday morning when very few people were even awake, a great thunderous clamour rang out from the church and it sank approximately twelve feet into its own foundations. Townsfolk said it had been an act of God that the church was empty at the time as less than three weeks before it had recorded an estimated attendance of over one thousand people for the funeral of a popular local man. Since it had been empty when it had fallen, it narrowly avoided becoming one of England's greatest disasters. In the early hours of July 9th 1788 and seen by only two living souls: a chimney sweep working a few hundred metres up the road who was said to have been badly shaken by both the sight and sound of the collapse and another man walking in Frankwell nearly half a mile away, who reported looking up just as St Chad's illustrious tower disappeared from view with a thundering noise amidst a great swirl of dust.

The problems with the church's state of repair were reported over a six-month period precluding its collapse. Among these various portents was the tale a week before St Chad's fall of a Vicar who was delivering the Sunday sermon when all of a sudden his hair appeared to turn sheer white. The congregation watched on in amazement as a silver cloud hung over the Vicar as if he was being lifted up to heaven in a shroud, but of course it was merely the dust cloud caused by falling plaster. One further omen occurred only two nights before the catastrophe: bell ringers were practising directly under the bell tower when they were showered with rubble and masonry. They quickly moved hymnbooks to the safety of the porch and reported the matter to the Vicar with a foreboding sense of doom. The following day the church elders convened to meet in the vestry with the County Surveyor of Public Works, a young man named Thomas Telford who they asked to survey the fabric of the church. Telford wore his tall hat as if taking a high attitude with them and before the meeting had inspected what he could of the church but then asked the elders if he could view the area under the clock tower called the Dimary (a place of the dead, full of coffins with very little light with a locked entrance for fear of grave robbers). The churchmen all went down into the foundations of the church, not trusting Telford to view on his own. He took quite a time looking around before they trouped back into the church for his summary verdict on its state. He explained the problem was a lack of maintenance. This brought a look of disdain from the elders who were informed that the problems dated back to when the foundations were first laid and the builders had simply not boiled the lime; thus in turn failing to allow the mortar to set at full strength.

The main contributing factor and one Telford was reluctant to mention was the blatant greed displayed in selling burial plots directly beneath St. Chad's, which over time had further loosened the already-weak foundations. It was a common custom for parishioners to request burial as close to the altar as possible, which many felt was nearer to God and would facilitate entry into Heaven itself. At the point of realising this Telford clearly warned them that it would lead to the eventual collapse of the entire building. The disgruntled elders requested what remedial action they should take and the best estimate of the repair costs. Telford informed them that a great deal of immediate work to the fabric of the church walls was crucial. In addition he pointed out that the roof would require a great deal of costly underpinning. Telford made sure to emphasize that the work needed to be carried out as a matter of urgency. Gathering to discuss this news out of earshot, the elders debated Telford's warnings and of course the matter of payment. Without hesitation, they took the decision to not only ignore Telford's caution but also to take time to search for a different opinion, in the hope of finding a more affordable estimate. They had further concluded that Thomas Telford had not long moved to Shrewsbury and may not be as trustworthy as a more local man. Nevertheless, in an effort to seem grateful and wary of their predicament they asked Telford how soon the work could be started and he replied, "If you wish to discuss anything besides the alarming state of this church, then we had better adjourn to some other place where there is no danger of it falling on our heads." With that said, they all made a hurried retreat to the side exit door and left to debate on the matter even more.

After their deliberations nothing further was agreed and less than twenty four hours later the bell tower collapsed, as warned, bringing half of the church down twelve feet into its foundations. This occurrence proved Telford right and secured his reputation in Shrewsbury from that point onward. The elders were now left with the far more costly debate of whether to rebuild anew on the same foundations or relocate completely.

"We do not know the exact price Thomas had quoted for St. Chad's restoration." Doctor Darwin informed his dinner guests, "but rumours abound that the cost of rebuilding St. Chad's from the original foundations upward came to more than £30,000."

King Eyton guffawed over his last morsel of Goose Pie and breaking the charitable Doctor's guests' polite silence, spoke out. "What a ridiculous sum for a mere church to attain! Where on earth could they possibly hope to get that much money!?"

Doctor Darwin presided over the table and a wry smile broke his lips…, "Mr Eyton, New St Chad's still stands tall to this day so you have to admit that the Lord does indeed work in mysterious ways..." The other dinner guests applauded the Doctor's retort raising a glass to the success of the tale. The now-humbled Eyton shifted lower into his seat where he remained silent for the rest of the evening. As the Doctor looked over the rim of his glass with distinct satisfaction, he recalled the omitted part of this tale that would have completely sated King Eyton's query.

This purposefully excluded chapter from the story of St Chad's fall and rise began with a patient of Doctor Darwin's whom he called upon in a late night visit shortly after his own first arrival in Shrewsbury. The call was to be made at Shrewsbury Castle which dominated the northern approach to the town. As the Doctor's coach approached the gate he was informed by a servant that the master was in a lower part of the fortification. Much of the castle was crumbling and had long since passed its halcyon days but the latest owner, the Member of Parliament for Shrewsbury William Poultney, had pledged to restore some of its former glory. As he descended a stone staircase the Doctor met a young man coming up from the dungeon area.

Speaking to Darwin in a Scottish accent he said, "Take care of the stairs and make sure you knock loud before you enter, as to give the master time to receive you."

Upon reaching the door the Doctor knocked and believed he heard a call to enter. The scene that welcomed him as he stepped through the door took his breath away. Sitting at a table, dressed in night attire was a man counting a huge pile of gold coins by the light of a single candle. To Darwin the man resembled a miser due to the manner in which his arm was placed protectively around the money.

Startled and enraged, the estranged man looked angrily at the Doctor, "Do you never knock before you enter a room?"

To which he replied, "Fret not, I shall graciously leave and return when you have regained control of your temper. However, I hasten to refresh your memory that it was you, good sir, who requested my attendance at this hour." He turned on his heels as if to leave but the man beckoned him back while covering the coins with a large white cloth.

"I am William Poultney and it is I who sent for you. First I must ask, you'll nay be staying will ye?" The Doctor knew the reason for this question and responded in the negative. As was customary when visiting a patient a doctor could elect to stay as a guest until he either diagnosed or settled the condition, which meant providing him with food. With the Doctor's famed reputation for eating already becoming legendary in Shrewsbury, feeding him often cost more than his fee.

"Tell me Doctor," began Poultney, "they say you always tell your patients the whole truth, going so far as to tell them that they are going to die."

"The truth does not hurt an honest man," said the Doctor, to which Poultney replied, "You shall be my Doctor on one condition only. You are never to tell me if I am about to die." For a man of medicine it was hard to change his ways but for the sake of conduciveness the Doctor agreed.

"Now whatever is the matter? You call on me as late at night as this but I have no right to take of your time," requested Doctor Darwin.

"I cannot sleep," said Poultney bluntly "and it has gone to such lengths that I have not had a decent night's sleep in an absolute age. Is there something you could relieve me with? I have fallen and stumbled a lot, I also have dizzy turns and last but not least, there is the matter of my hands." The Doctor could see them noticeably shaking when Poultney held them out for him to touch.

"I can give you something for the symptoms you describe," he announced, "but that will only send the problem away for the time being. What is it that's worrying you? We must look at what ails you deep within, not merely what is on the outside. Of course I shall have to examine you thoroughly as I have not seen you before."

"Not here." came back the old man, "Let us go up into my living quarters in the castle hall," which the Doctor was happy to do as with only the light of a solitary candle a thorough examination would have been nigh on impossible. Poultney shuffled to the door but allowed the Doctor to leave first.

The man shuffled repeatedly around the door and guided Doctor Darwin out on to the stairs, while he went back into the musty dungeon to put the coins back into the chest where his money was kept.

They went upstairs to the main hall of the castle which looked to the Doctor to be strewn with the wreckage of a battle. Debris from the breakage of furniture and windows was littered everywhere, other items of furniture had been turned upside down and there was the pervading, awful smell of night waste. "The waste of many days and nights," the Doctor thought to himself.

Despite the sickening odour, Darwin resolved to carry out the examination even though it seemed likely the man had brought misfortune upon himself. He asked for more candles to improve the light, to which William responded, "More candles?" as if not understanding the request.

"For God's sake man, I have to be able to see in order to examine you," retorted the Doctor angrily and with his patience fast evaporating added, "This is outrageous, I'm leaving." And for the second time that evening he turned to open the door when Poultney cried out for him to stay.

"My Doctor, this is what is wrong with me…. Money has taken over my life. There are people who would tell you I am the richest man in England. This may well be so but I live in constant fear of losing it all and have a great fear of spending money that will never return again."

He then rang for a servant who entered with an armful of candles. There was no hiding the Doctor's astonishment when the instruction came for the servant to light every single one of them. With the light rapidly improving, Darwin asked Poultney to strip and lie on a large table in the centre of the hall. He ran his eyes over the patient and asked him to carry out tasks such as lifting his arms and legs with his eyes closed and also placing his index finger onto his nose with his eyes shut. He took a small hammer from his bag and tapped William on certain parts of his body, listened to his heart and chest, making mental notes as he went along. The Doctor then began asking questions of the prone man.

"Where do you take your water from for this place?"

"From the river at the back of the castle" came the reply.

"Do you ever go to the country or take of fresh air?"

"Never."

"Do you ever have social occasions like dinner parties?"

"I have forgotten the last time I did anything of the like…I would guess the coming-out-party of my lovely daughter Laura, whom I no longer see."

"Small wonder" quietly thought the Doctor.

Poultney was asked to dress and take a seat while the Doctor considered his diagnosis. The patient looked intently at Darwin as he began to speak.

"I think you have a bad condition but at this stage it is not life threatening. I have noted that you are rigid and have a loss of reflexes. The shaking can be serious but curable. Your heart is sturdy and your blood flows strong and steady. I would like to remedy the short-term illness by prescribing some medication that you will obtain from Cartwright the apothecary on Mardol with my prescription." The Doctor sat himself down and began to scribe. "Now, I want you to listen carefully and you absolutely must do what I say every night and morning." He looked above the rim of his glasses and saw Mr Poultney shift uncomfortably in the candlelight, leaning in to listen with intent.

Poultney looked on in anxious anticipation. "You must drink a glass of hot water, as hot as you can stand. At breakfast the next day you will eat two eggs, both with the shell included. No alcohol is to pass your lips for the foreseeable future and you have to endeavour to take air at the nearest highest point at least once every two days. You must find the old well to this castle; they all have one and boil all the water you take from it before you drink it. Your diet will contain ninety per cent fresh vegetables. The rest of your daily meal shall be fish. I would also recommend that you put more air and light into this abode."

The Doctor paused and carefully drew a breath. He was about to instigate a risky strategy, one he knew would lead to substantial profit. As he went to speak, he could tell by Mr

Poultney's needy expression that he had no cause for concern. "I will now talk about your main concern of money. It seems to me you are worrying yourself into an early grave. The problem with most rich men is that, after a while, there is very little satisfaction to be had from the continual and unhampered spending of money. I think you should consider more charity work with this vast fortune you have amassed. There are many poor people worthy of your charity but rather than just give it to the poor, lend money to charity institutions. This venture is bound to bring relief to the stress you are putting on both your mind and body." Mr Poultney nodded incessantly, and it took all of the Doctor's willpower not to smile as he became aware that his subtle suggestion would work without fail. "Perhaps I could help you in this way with advice as to where to spend your money. I passed a young man on the stairs of the castle on my journey here. I believe I recently met him at the gathering to discuss the foundations for the new hospital where he was introduced to me as Thomas Telford from Scotland."

"That is correct, I know of him," replied William. "He is a man I have great faith in as both an architect and surveyor."

"Indeed," said the Doctor, "I happen to know of such a good cause in Shrewsbury. It is an old church in need of repair. By all accounts and religious connotations aside, there are many signs that if action is not taken immediately it will soon fall down. The church has very little money to pay for the necessary inspections. If, for example, an anonymous benefactor was to fund it, Mr Telford would be able to survey it for them and give his expert opinion. Given your insurmountable lending capability and my connections, should the church need extensive restoration, I am certain the satisfaction you would receive would last the length of your days. Above all else, the church is a worthy cause in need of donation, if ever there were one."

As Mr Poultney listened to the end of the Doctor's effective advice, his ears practically pointed to attention. He let out an overwhelming sigh and for the first time that evening, and for possibly a lot longer than that the Doctor hazarded, he sat back in his armchair and his tension began to visibly ease. The Doctor began to pack his case, as his work for this evening was done. Mr Poultney began to ponder the Doctor's advice and with a silent gesture the servants began to extinguish each lit candle around the room, and in the encroaching darkness the Doctor broke a small, knowing smile.

As Doctor Darwin left the Castle entrance, he made his way down the cobble-lined walkway and returned to his coach, a single thought blossomed in his mind. "The wheels are set in motion..."

After the dinner had concluded the ladies departed into the drawing room, where Caroline - the second eldest Darwin daughter - played pieces on the pianoforte. In the library the men settled to discuss the issue of the day: the war in Europe and the threat posed by 'the Beast of Europe', Napoleon Bonaparte. Most of them were of the opinion he should be captured and hung, with one going so far as to say 'hung until nearly dead, at which point his heart should be cut out and sent to the four corners of the kingdom'. When pressed for his opinion, the Doctor suggested he be exiled to a place where escape would be impossible, a notion that found little favour with his associates. Sir Rowland recounted the story of Napoleon's escape from exile in Elba, stating it was not a good thing to have him so near to Europe and according to Wellington "still in control of The Old Guard". Sir Rowland added that Bonaparte had an easy return to France, as things were not going well for Louis, the Bourbon King.

"Mark my words, we shall fight and defeat the Beast before this year is out," Sir Rowland stated confidently with the Doctor taken aback by the finality of his words. The Doctor continued listening to Hill with an attentive expression, although much of his rhetoric he had heard before. Soon enough though it was Rothschild upon whom his attention became fixed. The Doctor quite clearly noted that the banker hung on every single word that Sir Rowland spoke of the war, and its potential climax.

Later that night after the departure of many of the dinner guests, Doctor Darwin settled in front of his lounge fireplace with Sir Rowland and Nathan Rothschild. As the many hall-lights and chandeliers were extinguished the three gentlemen remained deep in conversation, only ever halting banter in the gas and fire-lit lounge to replenish their glasses and refill their pipes.

Following much small-talk, the banker returned conversation to the issue of the ongoing war in Europe. Speaking tentatively to begin with, Rothschild began telling of his escapades supplying money to Wellington's army in Europe. The money, raised in

England had to be smuggled to where the troops were and he told of gold coins being sewn into a great coat. Measures were even taken so far as to disguise men in the many layers of women's clothing in order to successfully conceal and convey currency. Rothschild said there were bands of deserters roaming around Europe looking for convoys of army gold to steal. After a brief silence he nonchalantly added, "Of course my brother Thomas does the exact same job, only he is in charge of fund-raising for the French side of the war."

At this very moment, Doctor Darwin's fascination turned to outright astonishment. The Rothschild brothers were on either side of this very war, with a foot in both camps. He had little time to ponder this revelation as the banker had resumed talking, saying that with Napoleon's return to France he must be defeated quickly as England could not sustain another long and costly war. Sir Rowland interrupted by saying, "Gentlemen, please remember Napoleon has never before engaged directly with Wellington and by all accounts the trap is set."

"General, to what trap are you referring?" probed the Doctor, "and where and when will this trap be sprung?"

Sensing that such a direct enquiry may prompt a curt and defensive response, Doctor Darwin raised a hand in acknowledgement to signify that no reply was necessary. However Sir Rowland, by this time of the night flushed with the flow of alcohol, was in no mood to remain reticent:

"Why, it is due to be sprung at a place called Waterloo, Sir." The Doctor's eyes grew in the firelight. The information that the General was giving him was just as incredible as it was priceless. Nevertheless the loosening affect of alcohol had taken the General and as he meandered in often broken sentences, both the Doctor and the Banker listened intently.

The General continued, "In all honesty the battle is actually due to be fought in a French town named 'La Havre Santé', but since Wellington believed the English would have problems with the pronunciation, the easily spoken name 'Waterloo' was selected to head up all plans. It is an area not far from Brussels. Wellington has already visited the area and decided that it will suit all best laid plans thus far. It will definitely take place in June of this year. I hasten to add that any man who can foretell the outcome of this battle could stand to make a lot of money, a fortune in fact. Oh yes, whosoever could garner the precise information, in a timely fashion, would surely make himself a very wealthy man here in England." The General's speech dutifully stopped its meander and his gaze became transfixed on the fireplace as his mind swam with inebriation.

Silence fell for only a few seconds but the Doctor's mind was ablaze. He considered all that he just heard, but without wishing to give too much away asked a mundane question of Sir Rowland in order to carry things along.

"I see that my very own old Mattie has retired from your service. Have you found a suitable replacement for him yet? If not, I do have an excellent suggestion should you need it?"

Before Sir Rowland had opportunity to reply the Doctor's mind had already begun working through the foundations of a lucrative scheme. Mattie was an old solider from Shrewsbury who had been with the General through every single one of his long campaigns, serving as his personal bodyguard. He had recently retired to his little house in Frankwell and was now working for the Doctor as his gardener. The house had once been owned by Darwin before he sold it back for a pittance to old Mattie, in recognition of the work his family had carried out in the service of the Doctor and his family over many years. Mattie's wife was in the household as were his daughters, while two sons worked on the Doctor's farm. Darwin considered Mattie's eldest son Matthew to be the jewel in the crown and everything he admired in a young man, with qualities he had not yet detected in his own two sons. He loved them both dearly but both showed a desire to play with the sciences, which often involved the creation of foul smelling gases, much to the annoyance of the people of Frankwell but due to their age the Doctor did his best to be understanding. Trained in all the skills of war, shooting, riding and sabre fighting, thanks in no small part to old Mattie's expert tutelage; Matthew had been in the patronage of the Doctor from an early age and with Darwin's money had been schooled by the finest teachers. Like his father and mother he spoke French and when Matthew joined the army, Doctor Darwin had helped him enlist in the Hussars. As he ran through these facts the Doctor's mind was a whirl of connotations and to himself he kept repeating the General's own words, "whosoever could garner the precise information, in a timely fashion, would surely make themselves a very wealthy man".

"Replacement bodyguard indeed" replied the General, with a more than a little slur to his voice, "Why, of course, who would you recommend?"

The Doctor was ready with his reply: "Why, Mattie's own son. He is a fine young man who takes after his father in many ways, is educated in even more and comes inbred with all the qualifications that you might require of a bodyguard," stated Darwin in a matter-of-fact manner. "He has served in the 14thHussars for the past three years. And I assure you he rides as well as any other man I have ever seen, shoots as if distance were no problem and uses a sabre as though it was part of his arm. In fact he has been my companion on the roads of Shropshire on many a lonesome night and put many a highway scoundrel to flight in my protection. Not only that but he also speaks fluent French; which comes from his mother's side of the family."

By the time he had finished speaking the Doctor saw the recognition on Sir Rowland's face. It was now the General's turn to make some silent notes, albeit slow ones at this hour. He spoke no French and that skill alone could be very useful to him if the war was won and France taken over. Having someone close to him speaking the language would be very beneficial. "The matter is done. I will word my man tomorrow," replied Hill adding, "and with that, my good Sirs, I'm afraid I must retire and bid you a good night." The ever silent banker mumbled a drunken confirmation and made to depart with General Hill.

As both Hill and Rothschild climbed the winding staircase to their rooms, the Doctor's mind was keen as a blade in spite of the late hour.

Already an expert at dealing on the London Stock Markets, the Doctor made particular and extremely profitable investment in ships sailing the trade routes to the Indies and Spice Islands.

Stock dealers knew him well from his shrewd profit making deals and the uncanny knack the Doctor's ships appeared to have of always arriving back on time. This was at a time when the present day success rate was only one ship in three returning on the due date with its cargo intact. Unbeknownst to the dealers Doctor Darwin was receiving intelligence reports supplied unknowingly by the

British Admiralty. The source of this vital information was a young officer in the British Navy, who as a young man had his life saved by the Doctor. As the result of an accident in a Naval dockyard he had lost a leg and was at the risk of gangrene but upon examination Darwin found it to be an infection he could treat. The Doctor's knowledge of the infection came from his time at the University of Leyden and as a result he was able to successfully treat and save the young Captain. But without the Doctor's intervention, the officer would have been left in the naval hospital to surely die.

From that very day onward he worshipped Doctor Darwin and supplied him with naval information regarding the movement of ships all over the world. All the Doctor ever had to do was pick a merchant ship that was going on a voyage with naval vessels sailing in the area, study its manifesto and destination and invest his money accordingly without unparalleled certainty. The naval presence gave cover from piracy to the Doctor's chosen ship and therefore he knew the importance of ultimate victory over France as England's naval ships were now masters of the seas after Nelson had defeated the French Fleet at Trafalgar ten years previous. This pattern of investment bought the Doctor fame at first, with many Captains thinking the Doctor was a good luck charm but City investors had their own thoughts. The Doctor had arrived at a secret way of investing in ships that was to stand him well in the future and it was soon known in London Stock Market circles that the Doctor's reputation for investment was down to more than just good fortune. The Doctor however had to cover his tracks when making an investment to ensure there was not a rush that would create an over-valuation of the ship, thus cutting Doctor Darwin's profit.

As the house steadily darkened and the fireplace dwindled, the Doctor himself decided to retire. As he laid his head to rest beside that of his wife he was already deep in thought, formulating his intricate plans, for the General had been unwittingly generous that evening. But just before sleep finally took hold he remembered one last thing from earlier that evening. Not long after the last of his two-dozen odd guests had arrived and while on his second circuit of the many rooms, he had stopped below the staircase in the foyer. He cocked his head and listened carefully as he heard the faint footsteps and giggles of his younger children as they ran playfully upstairs and avoided their curfew. He paused there that evening for just a short moment and pondered the innocence of childhood he overheard there. For many years to come after that, it never failed to bring an ironic smile to his face whenever he thought about the eventual outcome of tonight's gathering.

FOUR

Two Women of Shrewsbury

One springtime morning while at home in his office pouring over reference journals, the Doctor received a strange request from his coachman, Mark. Mark asked if he would pay a visit to a lady but was very secretive regarding her identity. The Doctor asked for information as he did of all new patients, but Mark seemed reluctant to divulge any detail at all.

"Mark, how can I possibly go and visit a person I do not know anything about. For instance, how could I possibly tend to someone if I do not even know where they live?" the Doctor enquired without even looking up from his desk.

Mark shifted uneasily and replied, "I apologise Sir for my being so secretive, but when you are introduced to the person I am sure you will understand their need for clemency."

The Doctor had taken many a strange patient in his time although never before had he attended a patient without full knowledge of their name and address. Nevertheless, he informed Mark he would go along with his appeal but only after they had visited a townsman Mr Tutpin, the local brewer and his daughter. Mark shuddered at the very thought of going to Tutpin's residence. This had been an issue for the Doctor in the past as it had on occasion threatened Darwin's social standing in the town. For all of the respect he had earned from the people of Shrewsbury over the years he had lived there, visiting this particular patient was still a matter that warranted the townsfolk's serious disapproval. Their cause for concern was that Tutpin's only daughter Sara had suffered from leprosy since she was only a child.

Tutpin also had a questionable reputation since his childhood when as a youth, he and his best friend Robert Clive had been members of a gang which terrorised the many butcher shops of Shrewsbury's own Butcher Row. The shops there were just open windows with wooden shutters, set upon releasable hinges that dropped down to form counters by means of pieces wood propping them up. Tutpin and Robert and the rest of their gang would knock the wooden posts away causing the counter and meat on the counter to fall onto the street. They would then run an infantile protection racket, demanding money from the butchers to make sure that it never happened again. They did go too far once and were taken before the magistrates in Shrewsbury. Tutpin and Clive were both convicted but due to Clive's father being a respected member of society, they both avoided prison (which is where most of the traders sincerely hoped they would be sent) but instead they were sent to India to "make men of them."

Before his time in India, Tutpin had already become well versed in the brewing trade and during his time there discovered that the available beer was both poor quality and weak by comparison. After several years of experimentation using the local ingredients, he eventually came up with an acceptable brew. But by this point his friend Robert had moved up in the world, to say the very least. He had made many connections during his rise through the ranks in the Army and the East India Company. Just as Tutpin finally perfected his brew it was of no small importance to his own career that his best friend Robert Clive of India was the single most influential representative for both the British armed forces and the East India Trading Company. Robert Clive of India was said to have returned to England as one of the country's wealthiest men. Robert and a crew of his own army contacts took a particular liking to "Tutpin's" as it was to become known amongst the soldiers. Following the meteoric rise of Robert in India, Tutpin went on to make a small fortune himself and came back to Shrewsbury and established his family business. About the town, Tutpin became known as a 'Nabob', a nickname specially given to those who travelled to India and returned with a fortune.

He had returned to England because the love of his life, his little Sara, had contracted leprosy. Tutpin always told the Doctor he did not know from where she had caught it, but Darwin knew enough to realise it was not from passing contact. Tutpin had often boasted of how his kind Sara was always going off to tell the local poor about Jesus' love and at times help them with their problems. In silence, the Doctor had already concluded this to be the most likely source of her dreaded disease. Life is so cruel, he thought. A young beautiful girl bothering to look after the poor instead of doing what most other young girls of her age were doing, namely pursuing a likely husband or honing her skills to obtain one. For this she was rewarded with the most foul of afflictions.

The Doctor had always informed Mark that he had nothing to fear from Sara since he knew leprosy was only contagious when you shared a huge amount of long-term exposure to the environment with the inflicted. By taking the proper precautions, as the Doctor advised, the illness would never be a threat to anyone else. Dr. Darwin had spent time treating and studying lepers in Holland. His mentor at that time, a Doctor Ling, told him that in his birthplace, China, there were thousands of lepers living in communities and that a necessary part of all medical training in that country was to assist in these places and help with every day illnesses. With this experience in mind the Doctor knew that when making his frequent visits to Sara Tutpin, there were certain procedures, instigated by Doctor Ling, which needed to be followed. Each and every time he examined Sara he would wear fine lined gloves and also a cowman's gown. His mouth would be covered by a very fine gauze mask to avoid breathing the leper's air, because from this the disease was most likely to spread. When finished he would fold the items carefully in brown waxed paper, take them home where he alone would boil them.

He arrived that day and began his regular examination of Sara. Immediately he found her to have a particularly nasty cold, likely picked up from her father, which had gone onto her chest and was causing a high temperature. The Doctor prescribed a herb for her, well known for reducing body temperature and recommended goose fat to rub onto her chest. He instructed that she must also continue having two eggs with shells every morning and if all was still not right after five days of the Doctors prescribed remedies, Tutpin was to send for him again.

As they came out of the establishment known as the Sextry and into the passage where it was located, they went out onto the High Street where the Doctor's coach awaited. The nearest thoroughfare to the Sextry was too narrow for Darwin's usual coach so he would normally use his smaller yellow single seater. The Doctor and his servants had fondly named it Sulky, since no matter the occupant, it always gave the impression the person in it was sulking, mainly down to the awkwardness caused by the constrained space within. Like his father, Erasmus Darwin, Robert had it altered to have space to carry essential things with him whenever he travelled. Unlike his father though, who took along books to read on long journeys, Robert Darwin made sure to stock his own Sulky with food for the journey to keep his great appetite satisfied.

Robert Darwin's Sulky was well known in Shrewsbury as, often on a late night he would fall into an over-indulgent slumber and people would marvel as his horse George would always find its own way home without any guidance.

After leaving the Tutpin residence, Doctor Darwin and Mark proceeded along Baker's Row. The Doctor still did not know the address to which Mark was taking him to meet this strange woman. He watched with intrigue as the coach turned up Pride Hill, going to the very top where it joined onto Castle Street. There, outside of Thorne's Hall, Mark stopped the carriage. The Doctor knew this to be the house of the Smythe family. In the past, he had treated various members of the Smythes, so he was even further baffled as to why a visit to this abode would ever need to be clouded in such secrecy. All was revealed as the Doctor was allowed through the front door and the house-servant, who had sent the original request to Mark to bring the Doctor, ushered them into the main sitting room. Lying there on a sofa was a very elegant and beautiful, yet unknown, woman covered with nothing but blankets. The Doctor reasoned that she was on the sofa because she was too ill to even climb the stairs and now lay where she had stopped to rest. He was greeted kindly by the servants as they took his cloak but still no name was given for the strange woman. There was no response from her as she lay with her eyes clamped shut. The Doctor was only given a brief explanation from the servant who mentioned that the woman had travelled a long way during the past twenty-four hours. At first Darwin thought she was completely unconscious; although it was now obvious to him that she was in fact very ill and slightly disorientated but awake nonetheless. As the Doctor drew closer to her, he immediately caught the scent of almonds surrounding her and gathered that she had either taken or worse still, had possibly been administered arsenic.

Dr. Darwin enquired again as to who this woman was to which the servant replied, "Sir it is not my place to say. I have already sent for the master and I'm sure he will have more information for you." Just as he finished speaking, a tall handsome looking, smartly dressed man entered the room. He apologised for the inconvenience and put out his hand to the Doctor, who instantly recognised the sign of a fellow Mason.

"Good sir, please allow me to introduce myself. I am Simon Beadle, solicitor and family friend to the Smythe family of Tong. These last two months I have been employed to serve as adviser and protector of this good lady."

The Doctor quickly responded, "Sir what part of protector were you playing exactly? From her current state I question that skill in particular. I demand to know just who this lady is, if indeed you ever want me to treat her."

As he had received the return sign of a fellow Mason, Beadle replied, "I cannot tell you the name until you agree both as another person of the Great Creator of the Universe and as a medical man not to reveal her identity to anyone outside of these four walls."

"On both counts you have complete assurance of my silence," said the Doctor. As Mr Beadle nodded the woman began to choke and writhe in pain. The Doctor stooped over and looked down at the poor woman. He reached down and touched her dampened yet ice cold brow. Turning to stand upright once again, the Doctor faced Mr Beadle.

"I do not believe it is in this mistress' best interest to wait any longer, so please do me a small courtesy and inform me of other facts relating to her present condition, such as how long has this woman been in this state? Have you noticed other signs besides her utter exhaustion?"

Simon hesitated and then freely admitted she had fallen ill only the night before. He then nervously ran through a list of symptoms the lady had been suffering from including stomach pains, diarrhoea, vomiting and convulsions. The Doctor examined the woman to confirm what he already knew he was dealing with. He gently took her hand in his and by studying the pigmentation of the finger nails came up with the confirmation of his fears. "Sir," he called to her supposed protector, "send for my coachman right away! I will also need the lady moved from this sofa to a comfortable bed directly."

Servants were called and the lady was moved. When Mark Briggs, the returning coachman, came rushing into the room he was told to go straight to Mr Cartwright in the Mardol to gain the Doctor a prescription. "If he can't provide all of the items on my list, tell him that the only two I require this instant are the powdered charcoal and apple pectin. Of all the ingredients I require Mark, do NOT return without those. Go with all speed and return henceforth. Move man, MOVE!" Mark jumped at the strength in the Doctor's voice and was off in a flash.

The Doctor followed in brooding silence as the woman was settled into her bed. He checked his pocket watch and told the maid to fetch a bowl of hot water, a funnel and soap, plus a cheese grater from the kitchen. As the maid left both gentlemen alone with the mystery woman, the Doctor then turned to Mr Beadle and quietly asked, "Would you now kindly take the time to fill in the details of this lady, as you are aware I have already vowed to keep the matter with the utmost secrecy."

"Doctor Darwin, I know of you from Tong Hall and your relationship with Mr Edward Smythe, also your reputation as a Doctor is known far from the town of Shrewsbury. In fact it is said at the Kings' court that if your father Erasmus Darwin had ever gone to London he would be the King's own physician."

The Doctor thought to himself that must be why his father would never go near London, as he knew about the jealous rivalry and backstabbing which were commonplace perils of the King's court. The malady bothering the King, as the Doctor's father knew full well, was not a condition of the body but one of the mind.

As hastily as possible and with quietened tone, Beadle began to unfold the tale behind this unfortunate woman. Her name was Mrs. Fitzherbert, a niece of Sir Edward Smythe, and Mr Beadle mentioned that the lady had even been born "in this very house". As he spoke about her recent "relationship problem" Dr Darwin froze with concentration, as her name made him recall her involvement in the news of late. Word had made it even to far-flung Shrewsbury of the recent Royal scandal concerning the Prince of Wales' rumoured illegal marriage.

Mr Beadle continued by saying that the Prince had great financial difficulties brought about by significant gambling debts and living luxuriously far beyond his considerable means. The

Prime Minister had recently made a statement that there was actually no marriage to speak of, as if it were a lie. Under even minute scrutiny that statement would have proven quite preposterous as the marriage in question took place in the ladies drawing room of a house in London and was formally witnessed by two reputable gentlemen and the Minister himself who had performed the ceremony. If the Prince were to prove that no marriage existed then the Prime Minister would gladly instruct Parliament to pay his debts. The thought of a scandalous marriage was causing great concern in the Royal household to the point of crisis, where the King feared for the future of the very Monarchy. There were strong feelings in the palace at that time and demands for drastic action were now being frequently heard.

At this point the Doctor interjected, asking whether this drastic action had been directed at Mrs. Fitzherbert.

Beadle's answer was immediate. "Doctor Darwin, that's why she is here in secrecy: to protect her life. We have brought her here in the hope that a fine doctor such as you can do something for her."

The Doctor thought very carefully and replied: "I am afraid it may already be too late. Tell me, was there anyone who made recent contact with Maria? Anyone at all that could have had the means to endanger her life?"

Simon thought about it deeply and replied, "There is one questionable soul whom I think may have motive and the means, a Mr Stangar." Darwin enquired who this person was. "He came into Maria's life only recently and is an agent for the establishment. I did not like the man from the start but he was very charming and wheedled himself into Maria's confidence." Beadle explained that Mr Stangar had told Maria he was there on behalf of the Prince to sort out new accommodation and had recently employed a personal maid for her needs. "That's when this problem started," said Beadle cautiously, "Maria was often sick after meals."

The Doctor drew breath and spoke; "There we have our answer. Someone has been poisoning her and that someone is more than likely this Mr Stangar, albeit surreptitiously through his maid. I must act with haste but I must remark again that given the length of time this has been occurring things do not look good for the young lady."

At this point the servants who had brought the items the Doctor had asked for retreated back into the foyer, giving Mark, who had just rushed into the house, room to enter the doorway. The Doctor called to the servants for one last item, this being a ladies commode. Taking the charcoal and mixing it with the hot water, Darwin left it to one side. Then he took the soap and by grating the block, made a thick lather in his hands, which he then added to a separate jug of cool water. He asked Simon to clear the room and when this request was adhered to he cajoled her into drinking the lather with fresh water, pouring it through a funnel. The Doctor struggled not to spill the potion over the incapacitated lady, as it began to make her retch badly, but with a steady hand he kept up the treatment until she began to swallow and within a minute of finishing the soapy drink Maria was being violently sick. He repeated the treatment over and over until it seemed there was no more in her stomach and then made Maria drink the charcoal mixture which promptly made her sick yet again. Despite her distress the Doctor kept forcing her to drink the potion and by now she had become wide awake and began fighting against the Doctor's applications. Gradually she settled down and became calmer. The Doctor now urged her to drink the apple pectin, itself an unattractive thick and sugary green-hued liquid. The lady did this and seemed to enjoy the taste. The Doctor told her and the servants that she must sit on the commode for the rest of the night and made double sure that a servant would stay and help clean her up. The Doctor then requested to be called every time Maria made waste, so he could observe it.

Darwin turned to Simon and reported this part of the treatment was now over and only time would tell if it had been successful. They retired to another room where the Doctor voiced a query.

"There is something bothering me, as to why the poison had not taken fully hold of her? Given the duration of her exposure she should have surely perished before I even had a chance to see her. Tell me Mr Beadle, does Maria fancy for a certain kind of food?"

"Why, yes Doctor," came the immediate response. "She is quite a glutton for cheese and never has any other drink but milk."

Doctor Darwin promptly asked, "Am I to presume Sir that she has had both of these in considerable amounts in the last few days?"

"Yes Doctor, they are her favourite treats," replied Simon. "She even had both on the journey from London to here."

"That," exclaimed the Doctor, "is the only reason she is still alive. So much for your protection Mr Beadle! You see the cheese and the milk would coat the stomach, not allowing the absorption of the arsenic. If the arsenic is present in her waste then we have a greater chance of saving her life."

All that night the Doctor stayed close by in an adjoining lounge, quietly sipping a drink of hot water in front of the fireplace. The rest of his evening, as and when necessary, he spent examining and smelling for the telltale signs of doom or recovery. Finally as night changed into day the Doctor was happy with his conclusions and shouted through the house, "Victory! She will live!"

Mr Beadle's pallid face broke a smile and the servants breathed a heady sigh of relief. As the Doctor collected his accoutrements he left one further bottle of remedial medicine which was to be given every two hours. "If it should run out before I return," he ordered, "you must send to Cartwright, the apothecary's store in the Mardol and refer him to my prescription which should then be repeated forthwith." As he moved toward the door the Doctor added, "I will see you later, Mr Beadle, to gain an update of the situation but only if I am not wanted by someone in further need of my services of course. She appears to be sleeping quite contentedly now."

That evening, after making his rounds, Dr. Darwin returned to Thrones Hall to find the lady sitting up in bed, still very weak from her ordeal but much brighter in disposition.

"Dear Doctor Darwin, I am told I owe my life to you, your skills and your knowledge."

The Doctor bowed, "Just doing my humble duty as I was trained Madam. But if I may be so bold, I should like to know from your lips what is going on and why this terrible misfortune occurred to one such as yourself."

Maria turned in her bed and asked that everyone should leave except for the Doctor whom she summoned to her bedside.

"I suppose Simon has told you of my predicament. I am sure that the Prince still loves me very much and I know that I love him. There is, however, the question of his debts. Of course, if he could remedy these I think life would be a lot easier for all involved. I do not condone his lifestyle but men wiser than I do say that love is made possible only through acceptance."

The Doctor cast a sceptical glance, which soon melted when he looked upon her pure beauty. His mind wandered as he thought about the ways he had of lending money through unhappy, married women. Taking all due care he replied, "Madam I know of a merchant banker in Manchester named Nathan Rothschild who is looking for a patron at the King's court. I am sure if the Prince were to contact him he would receive a welcome resolution to his problems. I would only be too happy to contact him on your behalf with a proposal. We could see what goes from there." Maria nodded delicately, her kind smile radiating more warmth than the roaring fireplace to their left. "Before I take your leave, Madam, I would love you to come to my house and stay as my guest. I would hate to think of you constantly relying on Mr Beadle's 'protection' skills." The woman politely declined, saying her stay in Shrewsbury has to be kept secret at all costs and a further move of residence would undoubtedly risk all involved. "Should you, kind Doctor, and your wife like to come here and dine I would consider it an honour." The Doctor smiled, then bid her adieu and made his long-awaited return home.

Two days passed and the Doctor and his wife paid a visit to Maria. By now, she was quite herself again, standing strongly as she greeted them both with affection upon entering the house.

After dinner had ended the Doctor was talking to Simon, with his own Susannah deeply engrossed in conversation with Maria who was filling her in on London, the latest court gossip and of course all of the latest fashions. Doctor Darwin and Beadle spoke of many things making sure not to mention politics and religion as these were topics that the Doctor always did his best to avoid. Time was spent however talking about the local gentry whom Simon knew very well.

He told the Doctor about the problems caused by a distinct lack of money amongst the gentry of Shropshire and its borders commenting, "They have plenty of land but little money."

This gave the Doctor something to ponder and after the cordial evening he left that night with more knowledge than he arrived with and he began to truly feel a powerful ally in Royal Court.

It was shortly after these two separate incidents that something happened to bring together these two women of vastly differing backgrounds.

The Doctor had been visiting Sara Tutpin on a regular basis but on one such day after he had examined Sara he realised she was beginning her journey to death. The sudden decline surprised even Dr. Darwin as he felt her health had been improving steadily since her last chest infection. Given an examination of her heart he had sadly found a discrepancy that was beyond even his considerable healing skills.

As if she could tell from his stern expression what was on his mind that day, she asked him to come closer than he ever had before and whispered in a weak and rattled voice, "I know I am dying but I have two wishes for which I seek your help, dear Doctor. I fear my father would never listen but a man such as you just might. Firstly, I would like to go to church this coming Sunday as other God-fearing girls my age do, in order to receive sacrament from the Priest and secondly I wish to be buried in consecrated ground."

The Doctor was taken aback by this request as he had always had a problem with merely treating Sara, but he knew the request had been made due to the collapse of the Old St Chad's church. Up until the church fell the Doctor had made an agreement with church elders and town dignitaries that Sara could live within the town, under the solemn vow that she never ventured out of her house at the Sextry brewery. By means of a passage over the road which adjoined Old St Chad's, it had often been said that when the Vicar gave a boring sermon the other clergy sitting close to the door would flee to the Sextry for a welcome drink. There was a passage over Kiln Lane which led into Old St Chad's by a door on the side of the main alter of the church and Tutpin had made an Oriole window so his daughter could sit and go through the service, safely guarded away from the congregation by a sealed glass window. Over the years this had caused great distress and anger to the people of Shrewsbury, for fear of catching the accursed affliction. If God

42

had smote the young girl, what right did she have to even come near the Church?

All involved had agreed to this arrangement in order to keep the peace as it meant that absolutely no contact was made with the young leper lady. Securing agreement for her to go to church and receive sacrament in person from the Vicar was an altogether different problem. Her request to be buried in consecrated ground also seemed an outright impossibility but the Doctor would as usual persevere until the problem was solved. His chance to do so came faster than expected as the elders of the fallen church decided to have a new church built as opposed to repairing Old St Chad's. The new church was built but where was the money coming from to pay the costs? Up to now all the contractors remained largely unpaid and were now anxiously waiting to see some return for their labour. The whole project came at the cost of the colossal sum of thirty thousand pounds for which they had very little collateral. All they possessed were just the ruins of an old church. It was for that reason they decided to call upon the Doctor whom they knew lent money. All the while the Doctor was taking care of the willing benefactor Old Poultney of the Castle who, under the medical advice of Dr. Darwin, was spreading his money in a more philanthropic way as a means to improve his health. Dr. Darwin approached Poultney directly for the money at a charitable three per cent interest rate and then proceeded to lend it to the Church elders at an affordable four per cent, which was a sound business move, with a guaranteed return for all parties involved.

Now the Doctor had to get them to help in the problem of Sara's final two wishes and that was not the only difficulty to overcome, as he had to explain to the elders that borrowing a vast amount with such little collateral could prove a tough task, but went to great lengths to say it might be possible if he used his influence.

He returned to them after a short but busy interval to say all was well but he had a personal problem that had taken up his time and their matter would have to wait. The elders were anxious to see an agreement on the money so they could get on with the planning of the new church so asked if they could assist with his problem and he began to tell of Sara's requests. Expecting their rejection of his plea, they surprised him by agreeing almost immediately. This took him aback and in a mood of mutual benefit he said, "We are all people of the same God as Sara and I would be much obliged if you were prepared to give your permission in writing."

The monies were exchanged and the new church was finished in due course. Sara survived on by the good Doctor's caring ways and under advice from his Chinese friend and colleague, Doctor Ling.

On the Sunday mass at the New St Chad's, Darwin and his family took their newly purchased pews at the front, right next to the Tutpin's. Sara was completely concealed in a great dark cloak with a veil covering her face. All went well until Sara went up to the altar to receive communion. The Vicar, who had not been consulted by the elders before this event, felt this was another matter where the elders had shown him complete disregard and harshly asked the verger to remove the unfortunate Sara from the altar. Darwin and Tutpin watching this, shifted uneasily since it was obvious they would not want the Doctor's deal to become public knowledge. Sara was turned away by the Verger and already an unsteady clamour began to come from the flock. The Doctor swiftly stepped up onto the altar, took her by the arm and gently ushered her back up towards the Priest. Dressed in dark fabrics and covered from head to toe, everyone became aware of Sara's presence. What had once seemed like it would be completed without report, suddenly made everyone in the entire church aware of Sara's presence.

The whispers grew until a young man who was sat closest to the front of the church spotted Mr Tutpin who was turning a steadily darker colour of red. At once the unknown man cried out in realisation, "The Leper Woman is here!"

At that moment, Dr. Darwin realised that this subtle ruse had been outed for all to see. The congregations worried whispers grew louder. The Doctor stood close to Sara and heard her whimpering sobs of fear. Indeed the Doctor himself began to fear for her safety. Dr. Darwin began to silently curse himself for placing a fragile young woman in such a dangerous position.

Panic and pandemonium were about to take hold when the great doors were thrown open and everyone stood in shock as two figures entered the newly set church walls. The two magnanimous figures began to take off their cloaks and the congregation fell as silent as a mouse. Standing with all the splendour of Royalty was the Prince of Wales in the uniform of the Knights of The Garter and on his arm was the woman of Shrewsbury, his rightful wife, formerly Miss Maria Fitzherbert who stood attired in the magnificent dress of a Queen. The couple proudly walked up to the altar and each took Sara by the hand. A quiet hush of sharply taken breath echoed around the church as Maria softly kissed Sara on the cheek and led her to the Priest unobstructed. Both the King and Maria stood over her as the wish was fulfilled. The congregation watched on without so much as a whisper while young Sara, in her fragile condition, was granted one of her final wishes. As she descended the altar followed by her Royal companions, quite off kilter for church protocol, a huge cheer went up followed by cries of 'God save the King.'

Sara was not laid to rest in St Chad's as the graveyard was not yet in use but instead in the churchyard of St Giles' church on the outskirts of Shrewsbury, which was said to have been a leper colony many centuries before. Doctor Darwin organised the payment for the funeral as a gesture of goodwill to Mr Tutpin.

All was well in good old Shrewsbury once more.

FIVE

The Boy With No Name

As Doctor Darwin made his rounds one day he came across the young road-sweeper whose life he had saved only a few years before. To look at him now, so fit and healthy, it was hard to imagine this same waif who had been heading for a slow and painful death, until the Doctor's timely intervention only two years previous.

The case had first come to the Doctor's notice soon after he had first built his now famous Mount House. Whilst sitting beside his fire of an evening the Doctor was earnestly checking reference journals and medical notes. On several instances that night alone the Doctor remarked how the soot fell into the fire from the chimneystack above. Like most men brought up from an early age to enjoy wealth, he had never beheld the sight of moonlit shadows cast by a chimneysweep and his boy before. Sat there that evening, the Doctor felt he should remedy this and decided to send for one soon enough.

Only a day later his own young Charles' scream pierced the peace of the morning air, coming from the sitting room of Mount House. "It's a boy! It's a little boy!"

The Doctor stalled halfway through his breakfast and ran through to the sitting room to see what was the matter. His children and servants were gathered around the unsightly mess and after sending them on their way he beheld a curious sight. Lying there in the hearth, the good Doctor did indeed find a small boy. Black as night from head to toe and clearly in terrible pain, it appeared that the young lad had fallen right down the chimney.

Doctor Darwin ordered his manservants to carry the small child to his surgery under the stairs. There he was wiped clean of the soot on his body and laid on a clean sheet for the Doctor to make an examination. He was around eight years old with a very small frame and had many burn scars. His eyes were bloodshot and swollen and all his finger and toenails were missing. The Doctor

46

now looked at the cause of the pain in the boy's leg. It was lying in a way that suggested it was broken; upon feeling it gently he quickly established where the break was. The child soon came out of the shock he had been in and began to scream in agony. The Doctor sent for his butler Edward and coachman Mark to hold the boy and upon further examination determined it was a clean fracture but nonetheless painful.

Darwin called to his eldest daughter Marianne who often acted as a nursemaid to his home based surgery, "My Marianne, please bring me splints, bandages and also a glass of brandy in hot milk."

Despite being a strict non-drinker of alcohol the Doctor knew it was the best way to make young children very drowsy and ease the trauma to follow.

When the hot milk and brandy had been brought to the boy and drunk, Darwin put the tiny child into a straight position on the table with his injured leg supported under the Doctor's arm in a lock, while the Doctor's two men servants held the boy steady. When he straightened his arm thus breaking the leg into a straight hold, Marianne placed the splints on either side of the leg and then wrapped the bandage around until the leg was completely covered. The boy was now unconscious and thankfully out of pain or harm.

The Doctor had treated many boys in his time but he had an instant affinity with this child in particular, a feeling very similar to when he treated his own boys. Whenever he asked the child who he was, the boy remained consistently mute. He ordered the boy to be taken to the servant's quarters and put into bed. As the Doctor washed his hands in a washroom on the ground floor, he pondered who the chimney sweep responsible for the young lad might be and what kind of man he was to abandon the young one after such a serious fall.

The Doctor enquired this of his butler who replied, "We hired Davis the sweep from over by the new Welsh Bridge."

"Send for him at once," he snapped loudly.

The Doctor thought very deeply all that morning about why he had never thought about these children used in this vile trade. It had never affected him before the way it did that day. The man would receive a tongue lashing about the conduct of this trade concluded the Doctor. It was commonplace for very young children to be chosen to go up chimneys because their bodies and bones had not settled or hardened and they could bend around the narrowest of chimneys. Sometimes they would get stuck and the sweep would light a fire at the bottom of the stack to force them up. Due to the chimneys being so tall, sometimes as many as three children were employed at once simply to use their hands and metal scrapers to remove hard tar and soot which had been deposited from burning wood logs and coal.

It was also common for a young child to become scared and reluctant to climb, so time and again an older child would follow behind and poke the feet with needles.

The Doctor knew all of this from his father who had crossed swords with many sweeps around Newark. In the worst cases his father had seen children who had contracted forms of skin and lung cancer caused by the corrosive soot and the constant burning of their skin. On some occasions the boys would even develop testicular cancer, which always resulted in the most excruciating and painful death.

Doctor Darwin did not come across a great deal of these problems as many of these children lived far from his reach in the very worst areas of poverty. That morning the true maliciousness of this trade against children dawned on him in a way he would remember for the rest of his life. When Edward, the butler, announced the arrival of Davis the Sweep, he brought forth a humble and diminutive figure dressed in a dirty suit. Davis stood looking at his feet holding a cloth cap which he held out in front of himself. He stood before Doctor Darwin who initially resisted a launching into a stern rebuke as he wanted Davis to provide as much information as he could about the incident.

"Well, Davis, what have you to say about this unfortunate matter?"

Davis replied, "It was just an accident. The boy must have lost his hold and fell. I'm sorry Doctor but I panicked and ran. I ain't never lost a climber before."

The Doctor was not too concerned about this incident as it was taken care of now but he demanded to know about the boy and where he came from. Davis replied by saying he had paid good money for the boy from a woman in Double Butcher Row in town. He told Darwin she resided in the house next door to Abbots House beside the Fish Street entrance and said he could show the Doctor exactly where to find her.

The Doctor took a deep breath and answered, "Very well Davis, for the time being I can tell you that this boy is staying with me, right here in this very house. Here he will remain under my protection until he reaches such a point in his recovery that I deem him fit to leave. You may return at a later date to show me where this boy's so-called mother lives. From here on in Sir, you will leave the boy's future to me."

The sweep turned to leave, knowing not to cross such an important man as Doctor Darwin.

Over the next few days the boy became quite the celebrity of the Mount House. The Darwin girls took to spoiling him as though he was a brother or a child of their own, and while the Darwin brothers, Raz and Charles, were somewhat reluctant to mix with him at first they did soon come round when he began to tell stories of his chimney climbs and told tales of their friends' homes in town that the boy had swept.

After the boy had been in the Darwin household for over a week the Doctor visited his mother at the house in Double Butcher Row, so called as the butchers had now taken to trading on both sides of the street. There were around fifteen houses in the same state of repair as this but upon entering the boy's home the Doctor was taken aback by the abject poverty before his eyes. The house was two storeys high and timber framed but had been much altered over years of bad keeping, with lopsided rooms added here and there to maximize the rentable value. It was now in such a poor state of repair that the building appeared truly unsafe and looked likely to fall over at any given moment. Darwin had seen many houses of this type during his years in Shrewsbury and very often they would burn down before they even had a chance of collapsing. Even with the 'storing of firewood' laws that now prohibited such in any domicile within the confines of the town centre, the law was still widely flouted, increasing the risk of fire.

The stairs in the house were badly dilapidated and even Mark the coachman on this one occasion hesitated in testing them. But when he deemed them passable the Doctor climbed carefully to a landing where a door was hanging from the frame. In the centre of the upstairs room was a bed with a live chicken standing upon it.

What appeared to be a bundle of rags beside the fowl moved suddenly, sending a bottle crashing to the floor. The bundle gave a distinct yawn and the Doctor realised this scruffy pile was his young guest's mother.

As the alcoholic liquor tainted the already foul smelling air, Doctor Darwin's hatred of the demon drink flared up and in anger he shouted to Mark, "Get someone here, a neighbour or something, to clean this hole of hers up and I will return shortly."

The Doctor took a stroll along the street past the row of butchers whose wares were all laid out on nothing more than shutter boards. There were short passages near these shops that butchers used for slaughtering and on certain days offal and blood would run down these passages. The Doctor mused on how hazardous this was to public health and how long he wondered would it be before people understood that dirt in meat and summer heat sped up the rotting process. The public would then stop eating the meat, which begged the question, why butchers did not think more about how they stored it? At Mount House the Doctor had an icehouse in the garden, which enabled them to keep meat fresh for longer. He knew much about the meat trade and knew first hand just how profitable it was as most of the butchers he knew could more than afford his services. The Doctor hesitated briefly before he passed the main butcher's stall, knowing that the owner once had his client Tutpin the brewer convicted and even brought a prosecution against the legendary Robert Clive of India for running a protection racket against the butchers.

In his typically sarcastic manner, Ned Blower, this particular butcher's proprietor asked, "How are Tutpin and that leper woman of his on this fine day, Doctor Darwin?"

The Doctor replied in a similarly insincere manner, "In good health, Mr Blower. That's why I have not seen him or his beautiful daughter lately." Ned was a patient of Doctor Dugard, Darwin's biggest rival in Shrewsbury. Both doctors mixed socially and shared medical information but Dugard was known as a bleeder, cutter and leech applier. Doctor Darwin disagreed with these methods of treating patients but he admitted that on very rare instances such treatments could be beneficial. Darwin had heard tell that Dugard bled and applied leaches to every single patient regardless of whether it was needed or not. Doctor Dugard preferred to go by the fancy name of 'surgeon' but according to Darwin, many butchers cut much better than so-called surgeons. In spite of Darwin's personal views, many other townsfolk held Dugard in very high esteem for the efficient way in which he seemed to practice medicine, which of course was a key element in keeping patients.

The Doctor turned at the end of Butcher Row and entered the coffee house that had set up only recently in Shrewsbury on the corner where it met Pride Hill. Coffee had become the new drink of the established rich, who were the ones who frequented these places. He sat down and was served a large cup of a rich aroma coffee that was often accompanied by biscuits. Darwin sat and read the paper that was provided for the use of customers in all good coffee houses. By now there were a fair few coffee houses in Shrewsbury and most secretly served alcohol as well, lacing the coffee with a choice of either rum or brandy. These places had been set up as an alternative meeting place for the gentry as gentlemen could not be seen in public houses. Papers or short-sheets were freely available and even a bible was on hand along with signs extolling the virtue of temperance. There was also a notice on the rules for gambling, which was permitted for low stakes. The coffee house Darwin chose to frequent was one that had stuck to the principles and traditions by not offering alcohol at all. The Doctor's coffee house was called Gibbons' after its owner Michael Gibbons.

Gibbons' coffee house also went by the name 'The Penny University', for on some days it would cost a penny to enter and one could attend an educational lecture or talk. The most popular lectures delivered were those given by Shrewsbury historian, the Revered Blakeway. Blakeway's sessions were always sold out, with both men and women attending and the Doctor always made sure he was a regular member of the audience. Doctor Darwin finished his coffee and made his way back to the woman's house hoping she and the room were in a more presentable condition. When he entered the Doctor could not believe his eyes as the room and the occupant had been almost transformed, as a request from Doctor Darwin rarely went unheeded.

The woman sat up in a clean bed and she herself had been cleaned to the point of freshness. The Doctor approached her but she shied away as though ashamed of her appearance.

He reassured her by asking softly, "Come now, my lady. What is your name, Madam?"

The woman simply replied, "Cook."

The Doctor came closer still and said, "Cook? You are William Cook's wife Ellie! My goodness, whatever has happened? I remember you so well; you were always a sober God-fearing wife and good mother to your children." He stopped for a second and thought, "I now know why the climbing boy meant so much to me: I was the one who delivered him and his sister into this world."

When he first came to Shrewsbury, Doctor Darwin found a potter's shop that took his particular attention. It was in the Abbey Foregate area of town, near to the bridge clay pit. The potter was a Mr William Cook and was already quite well known and very successful, since he was the first potter to ever stay permanently in Shrewsbury. Normally a potter would just visit a town, take orders, fulfil them, make their money and move on. William had seen the chance of regular trade and had so impressed the Doctor with his skills and business sense that Darwin would tell his father-in-law Josiah Wedgwood about William at every given opportunity. If he ever did forget to update him, old Joe would always be sure to ask after William as Joe too had started on the potter's wheel, but had never entertained setting up a shop to sell his wares.

Doctor Darwin looked at this haggard version of William's wife and spoke with a sad tinge to his voice.

"Tell me what has happened Ellie. I know the sad event of your husband's death but I also remember you decided to keep his little shop going and you had found a potter who was apprenticed to William to work for you. It was a while ago and I do not get to that part of town so often anymore. Whatever went wrong?"

Still in a haze of drink, she answered slowly but surely, "Doctor, it is a sad story. The potter I employed in place of my William decided to move on for more money and I could not afford to replace him. Things soon went from bad to worse without any income and my children and I were thrown into the street by our landlord. I had to sell both of my children to a sweep in Frankwell to keep myself going. The money has now been spent and I live every day waiting for the landlord here to throw me out. I have not seen either of my children since I do not know when and the bottle is my only companion in my fight against the hardship of life."

Darwin turned to Ellie's neighbour, who had helped tidy her up and said, "Here is a guinea. You are to take care of this woman until you hear from me. As and when the landlord does return, please tell him to contact me at my home. You are to feed and nourish Ellie and no matter what occurs, she is not allowed to have any alcoholic drink at all. Make sure she has boiled hot water every night before bed and two eggs in the morning boiled and she is to eat the shells complete. If you have problems getting supplies then you are to give my name and tell the trader to charge my account. I warn you my lady, stay true, you can only purchase goods for the lady or I will have you locked up and you will forfeit any reward I may see fit to give you. Do you understand?"

The neighbouring lady knew the good Doctor and his work for the poor of Shrewsbury and assured him his instructions would be carried out to the very letter.

The Doctor now took time to think the situation over carefully. He knew that his next course of action was to buy back the boy (whom he now knew to be named Billy) and at the same time he would also see Davis the sweep about buying back Billy's sister.

Darwin also put his mind to a scheme that would help the Cook family out of this terrible crisis. First and foremost he would see the landlord of Cook's old shop in Abbey Foregate, which had living accommodation for the family above. He would obtain the property on behalf of Mrs Cook and pay the rent for the first twelve months. For some time now he had heard tell that the Wedgwood factory at Etruia was allowing local merchants to have rejects from their kilns. These merchants were based only locally to the factory in Stoke and nearby areas. As of yet they were not on sale in Shrewsbury so as a matter of course he decided to arrange with the factory to deliver rejects to Ellie for sale in the town.

The Doctor was also an inventor and one of his many innovations was a night-light, which not only provided a light in the nursery but also served to keep a baby bottle warm. They were selling very well according to the Wedgwoods. The Doctor decided he would give Ellie sole rights to sell them in her newly leased store and the profit from them would go a long way to solving the family's problems.

For a while before helping Billy and his mother Doctor Darwin had been working to convince the Burgesses to make sweeping changes to Shrewsbury in the name of public health, which included widening the streets and improving the water supply. Knowing very well that if this was pursued they would have to borrow large amounts of money, with the Doctor their most likely lender, he thought this would be the time to offer a little something as bait. At the next meeting of the town council he proposed road sweepers should be employed to keep the waste off the streets and help people move around without soiling their shoes which would lead to an increase in trade. This made the councillors listen as all were connected with trade in some way.

"In fact," announced the Doctor, "I will pay for the first one myself. I know the very boy for the job, I know his mother very well. I even delivered the young lad with my very own hands. He goes by the name Billy."

At this point there were offers from most of those gathered there to sponsor a street cleaner. So by the time his leg had fully recovered, Billy became not only Shrewsbury's first street-sweep but also took charge of many other less fortunate boys. As dirty as a street sweeper might get, Billy was always mindful of escaping the clutches of "Davis the Sweep" and the horrid future the good Doctor had saved him from.

SIX

The Free Masons' Plot
April 1815

The Doctor was taking a leisurely nighttime stroll through the Frankwell area. It was a cloudless night and he enjoyed looking at the various buildings that comprised this small townland. History showed the Norman tradesmen took a liking to this area of Shrewsbury, giving it a French feel in architecture and layout.

The Doctor's favourite building in Frankwell, now on his right hand side, was "The String of Horses". It was a public house made from an old half-timber house, which was said in times gone by to have been the abode of the Bishop of Shrewsbury. According to the Doctor's favourite historical advisor, Rev Blakeway, the dates of the Bishop's alleged residence did not add up. The impressive public house had been built outside of the town's centre, as the confined places of Shrewsbury made it extremely difficult to erect any further buildings within the all-encompassing loop of the Severn. The houses were put together by matching numbers on the joints which were always scribed in Roman Numerals. The construction was able to stand on its own without any support and the walls were made between the frames. These in turn were filled with wattle; a daub wattle being a basketwork of interlaced sticks filled with a mixture of any wastes such as dung soil and straw. The old wooden frame establishment was covered with the telltale signs of Shrewsbury's rope-like decorations. Moulded onto each front was a robe-like adornment, displaying the traditional quatrefoils: clover shapes or four-leaf flower carvings. It was said that the more timber in the building meant it was older, as both Henry VIII and Elizabeth I cut down most of the recent great oak forests to build naval ships. After these sudden and long-lasting local deforestations, considerably less oak supplies were available for building and at the time of the erection of these ancient buildings oak was the main wood source used.

As he walked down the hill to the foot of the old Welsh Bridge he entered another old timber-based structure known as The Fox Inn. It was here the Shrewsbury Masonic Lodge held its meetings. The Doctor remembered his initiation to the Masons at his mother lodge in Newark. The sight of blood used to be something that caused him great distress to the point where he could scarcely endure being in the same room as someone 'bleeding'. Unfortunately this was a practise still carried out as a method of healing. It was still very much to the disgust of the learned Doctor who knew it to be a meaningless procedure and that it made no difference to a patient's health whatsoever. However, the Doctor often pondered that if it succeeded in making a patient feel better then who was he to stop such ignorant acts administered by charlatans, quacks and even barbers. The most the Doctor could do, and never failed in fact, was merely to advise all and sundry that such a treatment was medically meaningless. At the meeting when he first became a Mason, the Doctor's eyes were bandaged and his coat sleeves turned up for the ritual. He knew that an important part of his vows was his intention to shed his own blood should he ever betray any fellow Mason's secret. As he was led through the initiation, he swore he felt blood trickling down his arm and could hardly believe his own eyes when after the clandestine ceremony he could not find even the smallest prick on his skin. Fear, he thought, had the ability to play very strange games with the mind.

That evening, as the Doctor ended his evening stroll and entered the room set aside as a Masonic temple, he beheld all the associated trimmings of Masonry on display about the room: the square, compass and of course the all seeing-eye. Walking through the oak doorway he surveyed the assembled Masons; there present were some of the most important men in Shrewsbury. They came from all walks of life and were specifically chosen for their honesty and trust. Tonight of all nights, these traits would be tested to the limit.

The Doctor addressed the meeting by saying that due to the war with France everyone present was far better off than before. Indeed, most had become extremely wealthy from dealing with the army who required regular supplies of wheat and general foodstuffs, the sale of which had been handled by the Doctor through his very good friend Lord Hill who acted as Quartermaster to Wellington's army.

Every man in the room listened intently to the words that came from Doctor Darwin's lips.

"Gentlemen, what I have to say could present great consequences to your future health and happiness. Anyone who does not want to risk all, including their life, will be excused from this meeting."

Not a single man moved, primarily because all present had done well out of past plans carried out at the Doctor's instigation. He explained his idea of going to London on what would be called 'a celebration of their good fortunes due to the war'.

"While in London, we shall visit the stock market and you will buy on my recommendation. I would like you all to be quite intoxicated by the time you first arrive there on the first day." This was met by guffaws of surprise, as he was known to hold very strong views about abstaining from alcohol, views which most of them had heard often. "Do not question my motives, but you will buy some very unworthy shares on my advice on that first day, but the next day when they think you are stupid, you will buy even more. This may sound strange but all will be revealed. That is all I can tell you at this stage. I stress once again that silence on this matter is of the utmost importance. Therefore, gentlemen, I must ask you to take the Masonic oath of silence once again." At which point the Masonic gentlefolk of Shrewsbury all spoke aloud and in unison, "May the great architect of the universe cut out my heart while I am still living and show it to me, should I ever break this oath of silence!"

After the meeting had ended, only Thomas Eyton approached the Doctor to inquire an estimate of how much money they were set to make on this venture. "That," answered the Doctor, "depends on how good you are at the task I set."

This inquiry worried the Doctor because Eyton was prone to spend money freely and live well beyond his means. In the position of Receiver General of Taxes for Shropshire, Darwin had certain suspicions of Eyton, as the tax collection system was wide open to potential abuse. Also the Doctor found it hard to trust men of the Church who took the oath of the Masons as he knew they only answered to one God of the Universe.

On his stroll back up to Mount House later that evening, the Doctor's mind wandered far from monetary matters and back to the townsfolk of his beloved Shrewsbury. Scanning the environment that evening he focused on the people of Frankwell and what he had learned to his own cost when he first moved here in 1800:

They were a very proud people and did not take kindly to charity, but Frankwell was renowned as the poorest part of Shrewsbury. Given their apparent destitution, the Doctor, in an effort to please his wife, let it be known to the limited population of this impoverished area that he would treat them for nothing. He was incredulous when nobody took up the offer but Anne, his cook, explained their pride so he came up with the arrangement of giving them medicine in a bottle, telling them there was a penny on its return - this was after he charged a penny for treatment. It was a system that suited both parties and from it the Doctor gained the unofficial yet grateful title of 'the father of Frankwell.'

SEVEN

The Hussar's Wedding

Mattie Matthews, son of the Doctor's recently retired old coachman, was a fine figure of a young man. He had been known to the Doctor literally all his life as he had delivered him and was always interested in how Mattie was getting on. As a boy he had looked after the pigeon loft and had by now grown into a specialist on these birds, and become most adept at breeding and nursing them. This had not only endeared him to Susannah but also to the Doctor, as Mattie's knowledge of carrier pigeons had allowed him to send the Doctor various confidential and urgent messages on his many trips away. On many a long journey the Doctor, his coachman Matthew and Matthew's young son, had taken pigeons as their sole companions. On such journeys the youngster would show his skill at looking after these clever little birds and never failed to constantly deliver what was termed "a returnee" - a carrier pigeon that never failed to arrive home. Darwin soon grew a great affection for this young man, based on his kind and humble yet capable nature. In fact the Doctor often treated him as a son, going as far as to pay for his training in the art of sabres and pistols (of course with express permission from Matthew). The Doctor was inwardly hoping that when he was ready, Mattie would take over from his father as coachman. In time though it became evident that this would not transpire as Mattie decided to join the army.

Soon after his meeting at the lodge the Doctor sat in the office of his surgery at Mount House awaiting Mattie, whom he had sent for, to explain the task he wanted carrying out.

As the young handsome man entered his office, the Doctor could still not get his breath at how much he had matured. "Mattie" he asked, hiding his consternation well, "when do you return to duty?"

"As soon Doctor as I have achieved the reason for my coming home from the army, that is to marry my fair Alice Ann. She is a dairymaid on your farm. I am led to believe by my father that you have a request of me, something to do with my posting in the war."

"Well," revealed the Doctor, "what I would like is for you to take a pigeon with you to war. You are to keep it, protect it and in time will come the order to release it. I will tell you no more. In this matter, the less you know the better. Do you think you would be able to undertake such a task?"

Mattie was the one now taken aback, as it seemed such a ridiculous thing to do but all the same his unshakeable loyalty to the Doctor meant that he could never hold back on agreeing. Mattie nodded dutifully and the Doctor dismissed him.

In the morning room of Mount House a few days later, the Doctor assembled his own family plus old Mattie and his wife. With its double winged library boasting marble columns that sustained the high ceiling, he asked them to close their eyes. When they were allowed to open them, standing there was the majestic figure of a hussar dressed in full regimental colours. To gasps and cries of amazement the two boys, Charles and Raz, began jumping for joy until Mattie reached down and lifted both of them onto his hefty shoulders. Upon doing so, he marched from the room into the glass conservatory carrying both aloft while keeping a steady pace as he went. He then moved onwards into the drawing room where Caroline, Doctor Darwin's second daughter, provided accompaniment on the pianoforte with the rousing song, "The British Grenadier."

On many occasions over the following years, the Doctor would sombrely reflect that such was the scene played out many times in the days of the Napoleonic Wars: laughter and merry-making swiftly followed by sorrow and death.

Not long after his agreement with the Doctor, came the morning of young Mattie's wedding. The wedding party met at 'The Bull in the Barne', only 400 yards from Mount House, a venue notorious for clandestine marriages. The Bull, as it was known locally, was said to stand on once-consecrated ground. As a result local people who were without the necessary time or approval to receive the official blessing of a marriage (a servant marrying above their station for example) often used it as the location for illicit weddings. The service of Mattie's wedding to Alice was conducted by a retired clergyman and on this occasion time was definitely against the couple. Mattie and Alice were accompanied by both sets of parents and also the Doctor, acting as reputable witness. Alice wore her mother's wedding dress, white trimmed in red, which in those days signified an unmarried girl.

The room was small, furnished by just a table which served as an altar. It was not the sort of wedding Alice had imagined for herself, but circumstances overcame the occasion and while pondering these thoughts it came to her notice that none of her fellow servants were present. But Alice chose not to dwell on these matters for too long, concentrating instead on her pride in Mattie, dressed in his Hussar's uniform topped with his black Busby. She was also surprised by the Doctor's presence but that was his way, always showing kindness and consideration toward his servants. The service was short, succinct and only made legal when both parties said 'I Will', followed by the traditional kiss.

When Alice came out of The Bull, her breath was taken to the extent she almost fainted. There to greet the newly-weds were all the household servants and to her utter delight, so were Mrs Darwin and all of her children. Everyone cheered as the couple came into view and through her tears Alice spotted the Doctor's coach, draped in red ribbon and edged with white to define a married woman. Mattie took his wife by the hand and helped her to climb into the coach, without having the slightest notion of where they were bound. The coach headed down the Welshpool Road, past Mount House, over the Welsh Bridge, up Mardol and Pride Hill then down Ox Lane and Dogpole, coming to a halt outside The Lion Hotel. Alice and Mattie were shown into the bridal suite and this caused Alice to shed more tears, as Mattie pointed out that this was the doing of the Doctor but did not divulge what their benefactor had asked of him in return.

The couple came down the stairs and were shown into the Lion room, where a wedding breakfast was set out for them and their guests. Alice took her place at the table and all the guests were introduced one by one, starting with the lowest of the Darwin household, the scullery maids and moving up to the butler Edward and finally the Darwin family members, Marianne, Caroline, Raz, Susan, Charles and of course, Mr and Mrs Darwin.

The Doctor had arranged and paid for the wedding celebrations but on his way to seek out the owner of The Lion to thank him and receive the bill, he met the only person capable of dampening proceedings, the most dreadful gossip ever allowed to walk the world, Catherine Plymlcy. Many times she had tried to find something that would have him at her disadvantage, but the Doctor thus far had always remained one jump ahead of her.

"Robert Darwin, I know you have always looked after your servants but this goes a little too far, even for you. Why are you willing to offer such a generous gift to *this* married couple?" The Doctor knew he would need a viable answer to satisfy her curiosity but remembered what his solicitor Mr Pemberton always said, "if a question took you by surprise, fake a fit of coughing until you can think of a reply." As directed, he took some time before offering his reply, "Madam, I do not like to think the people of Shrewsbury having short memories of our war heroes, therefore I do what I can for our solider boys."

Once again Catherine knew she was beaten to the gossip by the Doctor and he stepped around her to continue his search for the owner.

Later that night, Alice lay in Mattie's arms and revealed to him her recurring dream, one about a coffin with Mattie's name on it. In her dream she could see the coffin lid was open but when she peered inside it was empty. This troubled her greatly as she knew the perils of war that Mattie would surely have to face in the not too distant future.

EIGHT

Eleven Men Take A Trip
June 1815

The Doctor was soon making plans for the Masons' trip to London. He had made the journey many times and knew where to stay in London but as this excursion involved ten other people, he had the problem of guiding coaches to the address. As they were all Masons, it was decided that they should travel under the guise of being part of 'a farming community' in order not to bring undue attention to themselves. Their chosen method of transport, not befitting gentleman of their standing, played a big part in their plan to travel incognito. The 'poorman' guise was an added element of the Doctor's plan that eventful day. The owner of The Lion Hotel had established a reputation for running coaches from Shrewsbury to London and as a long-time Mason himself, would actually be among the party. This would no doubt assist greatly in the outward perception of them being nothing more than a group drunken Shrewsbury farmers, as he had become very familiar with this sort of behaviour in running coaches to and from the many Shropshire markets.

The Doctor arranged for the party to gather at Shifnal, some fifteen miles from Shrewsbury, to prevent any suspicion being aroused within the town itself. They met at the house of a patient the Doctor had once treated, a man who could be trusted to provide the necessary clothes that would transform the wealthy into lowly farmers. From here they would continue the journey to London and stay at the "Swan with Two Necks" in Ladd's Lane near the financial centre of London, where Doctor Darwin was well known in his alternative life. The Doctor met the party that evening as they sat down for dinner following their arrival at the inn. Ringing his empty wine glass for silence with a fork in his customary fashion, he laid out plans for the coming days. The ten Masons listened with ears pricked and breath held as he unfurled the next stage in their coup.

"On the first day, you are to arrive at the stock exchange at around 12.30pm and each of you is to appear in an intoxicated state. You must proceed separately and buy the stocks I have listed for you, making great play with the bag of money I have provided. I then need you to go into great lengths and tell all who will listen of how well you have done from the war, selling goods to the army." He was insistent in telling them not to worry when initially the stock they purchased did badly, as displaying to the dealers their idiotic tendencies was key to the successful implementation of his plan. As his team nodded in careful agreement the Doctor went on: "The next day you arrive at the exchange you will behave as if still under the influence of drink, but at all times you are to keep a clear head. As soon as the Stock Exchange reaches its usual state of frenzy, I will at that time give you all quite a substantial amount of money and also letters of credit from various banks. This you will use to buy consuls or Government gilts. Look for me standing by the great pillars and when I place my hand on my head, buy as many as you possibly can. Tell the jobber the code word is 'Big Bob X20'. You might even be able to purchase the consuls directly from desperate dealers."

Looking at their transfixed faces, he continued: "When you have spent all of your money, head back for the Swan but make sure you take great care of the certificates or receipts that you have for your freshly purchased consuls."

After leaning so close as to feel the Doctor's very breath, all of the Masons leaned backward into their seats and breathed many a quiet sigh of relief. The plan was simple enough and as the gents took their time in lighting their pipes and reordering flagons of ale, the normal course of conversation soon resumed. The Doctor watched his team of operatives with a knowing eye, as this was more than a mere investment. If caught, they would all be charged with treason. As the night wore on and conversations roared, the Doctor took a quiet second and placed his faith in the Masonic oath as it was the only thing guarding every last one of them from the hangman's noose.

NINE

Bertie The Waterloo Pigeon

Mount House housed a fine pigeon loft and throughout her life Susannah Darwin, both in her original home in the Wedgwood household and later here with the Doctor, loved this particular breed of bird. The Doctor garnered a fascination with pigeons due to their unique ability to always return home. The information he used them to convey would always gave him an important edge in business. What the Doctor failed to ever interpret from these dutiful emissaries was their unknown ability to garner their own thoughts. One particular pigeon that eventually made the Mount House roost his home had significant views to share:

"My name is Albert but I am known to my friends as Bertie, from the Prince of Orange and blood of Hanover. The first thing I would like to clear up about animals is that some of us were given the gift of hearing and understanding but not speech. Humans think we do not understand what they are saying, but how strange then that they always talk to and confide in their pets.

I am a carrier pigeon and have been in the service of Doctor Darwin for little more than 6 years. The places he has sent me to are nobody's business. At this very time my main concern is the latest trip I am about to undertake for him. I do hope my destination is not Spain as I have found that place to be very hot on my journeys and the heat does ruffle my feathers ever so. There has been much speculation about how I find my way back and while I cannot speak for others, it may have something to do with the way my owner, the Doctor, always takes me to my loft in London before any of my journeys. There he lets me mix with my hen Hattie but is most careful not to let us go so far as to mate. Sometimes the Doctor also lends me out to some people called the Rothschilds. They are always glad to see what I bring in my message and I always get to spend a lot of time with Hattie afterwards. The Doctor says that when my days are done he will take me to a place called

Shrewsbury and put me in the finest loft ever with as many hens as I desire.

On a more serious note, one night of late the Doctor came to my loft and told me a Masonic story. As the Doctor had been to the highest offices of Masonry the things he said had been handed down through the ages. It seems that Alexander the Great when he conquered Egypt was told a story known only to the Pharaohs. Their Gods used pigeons not unlike me, to take messages around the universe and because of the great distances involved they used what the ancients called "Holes of Black". These are tunnels, like shortcuts, making travel quicker and easier, if only we had them here! These holes in space were not only shortcuts but could be used to send back messages to the past giving people there the power of seeing the future, a trick I am certain the good Doctor would love to one day master. The Doctor, contrary to what he practices with me and my Hattie, believes that other pigeons today still use these 'Holes of Black' to guide them home so accurately. He told me many stories that at various influential times in his life Alexander the Great used pigeons in his campaigns which always gave him the advantage in intelligence and no doubt helped secure many a victory.

I don't know anything of the 'Holes of Black' but I have faith in my owner as he confides in me so much and treats me so well. Is it any wonder why I always manage to find my way home?"

TEN

The Battle
Sunday, 18th June 1815

Mattie picked up the pigeon from its loft close to the Stock Exchange and headed by horse towards Dover. He did this on what was no ordinary horse, it was a jet-black Spanish stallion renowned for his strength, bravery and high spirit, which had been given the dubious name 'Devil'. It was the finest in the good Doctor Darwin's stable. From the Dover coast Mattie sailed to the port of Ostend and after leaving the ship, made his way with an army convoy towards Brussels.

The Commanding Officer of the convoy had received an order to rendezvous at a village on the Brussels road where the army were collecting its strength, at the place revealed previously by General Hill to Doctor Darwin at the Mount House dinner party. Mattie was to find out where the field Headquarters were established and to make contact with General Hill. Wellington had chosen this spot as he recognised this location as the perfect place to deploy the same tactics that had proved so successful against the French in Spain and Portugal.

Hiding his main force behind a slope was a policy quickly embraced by the British soldier. Not only did it hide the true strength of the British forces, it kept the army out of range and aim of the French cannons. Up until that point in British Military tactics the British troops had been easy prey for musket and cannon fire with their 'stand to meet your maker' tactic of standing in columns and confronting an enemy head-on in the open. This school of thought had inflicted insurmountable casualties upon Wellington's men in the past and he had learned this lesson well.

Wellington had set up his command post at a small inn on the outskirts of Waterloo's pivotal battleground. When he arrived, Mattie reported to General Hill and was ordered to take up a position at an old chateau called Hougoumont and issued instructions that the farm and its surrounding buildings were to be fortified.

How little Mattie knew at that moment just what an important role he would come to play on this day, in the greatest Battle that the British army had ever fought. Unwittingly he had been positioned on the right side of the British line and Wellington had some intuition that Napoleon was likely to attempt to breakthrough there.

As the sun grew higher in the sky that day, the French army did arrive as expected. The two mighty armies drew up facing one another, waiting for the rain to stop and the terrain to dry. It had been raining throughout the last twenty-four hours and one hundred thousand men were sure to churn the ground quickly into a sea of mud.

Later, after being summoned to Headquarters, Mattie took his place by the great Duke and marvelled at the figure of the man that he was, standing tall and dashing in full battle regalia while bearing finely coiffed dark hair and sporting a great hook of a nose. Much to the contrary, this nose added to his looks and charming manners and helped not only to intimidate fellow gentlemen but also made him extremely popular with the ladies.

"Come hither, my highly recommended companion," said the Duke to Mattie, "I require you to take a message to the Prussian leader." The Prussians had been routed by French forces under the command of Marshal Grouchy the night before and Wellington was anxious that he keep his word and come to Waterloo as soon as possible. Napoleon on the other hand knew it was imperative to keep a force between the Prussians and Wellington to prevent them coming to the aid of the British. The Prussians, led by their notorious Commander Blucher, arrived at the battlefield unhindered as the Rothschilds had bribed Grouchy to allow them access and in doing so sealing the fate of the Beast of Europe.

Laughable news soon reached Wellington's Headquarters that Blucher had fallen from his horse and had lain trapped for most of the previous night. As soon as he heard this, Wellington briefly looked up from his plans and maps to give the following reaction, "I suppose he was pissed again."

Blucher had the reputation of suffering from the worries of war and was often found significantly inebriated on the battlefield.

Some years later he went quite mad and when he met Wellington again said he had been raped by an elephant and was apparently with calf. On this, the climactic day of the Battle of Waterloo, Blucher had promised to come as early as time would allow but remained dubious of Wellington's true intentions given the atrocious weather, which led him to believe the British may turn and run for Brussels. It was for this reason, therefore, that Wellington made sure that his stalwart colleague Mattie was sent to reassure the Field Marshal.

The battlefield was criss-crossed all of that day by men on horseback carrying messages to and from the various drop points. From these points the messages could then be hand delivered safely. Traversing the quietened battlefield as it took time to dry Mattie did not have to travel far on the back of his Devil ride before coming to the specific point where messages were being sent to the Prussians and so, upon arrival, he passed his vital message onward so that he could return to the Duke's Headquarters with due haste. This method of communication was to contribute greatly to the winning of the day as Wellington had the advantage of knowing where and what his forces were doing at any given moment. This practice was precisely the opposite of that relied upon by Napoleon, who left his Generals to obey strict guidelines of conduct and use their own initiative whenever the tide of battle required. By the time of Waterloo though Napoleon had a shock coming in his direction, as his generals were either getting too old or were quite fed up with the rigours of constant war.

All Mattie thought of on his swift ride back to the Inn was safely squirreling away within Wellington's Headquarters and quietly awaiting the outcome of the battle without fear of slaughter. However, this intention was not to come about quite as easily as he had hoped on this troubled day and unknown to him, Mattie was destined to have an extremely busy time on the battlefield of Waterloo.

No sooner had the two great armies faced up to one another than the familiar barracking began. The British sang songs about Wellington: "Who's the man to kick Bonie's arse? Our man Harry! Who's the man with a hook in his nose? Our man Harry!"

And the French hollered out in recourse 'Bonie beat the Prussians, Rah, Rah, Rah."

Suddenly a great cry went up from the French followed by a shout from one of Wellington's officers.

"Sir! Here he comes!" and up rode Napoleon on a great white charger. The officer who spotted him called to Wellington, "The Beast is within range, shall we shoot?"

"Commanders of great armies have better things to do than go around shooting each other," came Wellington's curt reply. "Let's watch him being adored," said Wellington, as any delay in time suited him just fine. Knowing as he did that the sand in the hourglass was trickling and that the ground was slowly drying, even so, time was still on Wellington's side. Wellington's Headquarters in the old inn was situated on a crossroad and the whole area was a seething mass of officers. In total 50 men were at Wellington's direct command and this included a very proud Mattie. Wellington invited all of them into the battle conference, having started with Hill. "Gentlemen," said Wellington, "we must hold Hougoumont with tooth and claw. We have to delay the battle long enough for the Prussians to arrive. The Commander of Hougoumont is a powerful Highlander by the name of MacDonnell and I have told him he has to defend his position to the very last man, no matter the cost. I would send more help if I could, but it all hangs on what Napoleon throws at him." Looking directly at Hill, Wellington then spoke, "At a time of my choosing, I want your man to go to MacDonnell directly with a message. So pray tell, Lord Hill, what is his name again?"

"Matthews" replied General Hill.

Mattie had stood outside the Headquarters waiting to be called for what seemed like an eternity, waiting for the command to act. He looked over the battlefield and was mesmerized by the colour and splendour of the opposing armies who manoeuvred to the sound of bugle and drum. But this was not a pageant, it was a battle and soon men and horses would be falling to their death to the sound of a different concord. Awestruck by what he beheld, he was suddenly startled by a voice that commanded: "You are to report to the General forthwith, Hussar Matthews."

Shrugging off the startling surprise, Mattie followed the smartly dressed soldier back into the Inn and to the desk of the Great Duke himself, as Wellington was widely known among the ranks.

"Matthews, I want you to go straight to Hougoumont. There you will find Colonel MacDonnell and communicate this exact message: I can spare no more men and I expect him and his men to serve with honour, making sure to fight to the bitter end should it suffice the outcome of this battle. The Prussians will arrive in due course. God save the King."

Mattie trudged over to Devil, his steed, and after mounting looked across the battlefield and worked out the best route to Hougoumont. It would take two miles of crossing various infantry and artillery formations to reach even the faintest path leading to Hougoumont. As they hurriedly wended through the skirmishing soldiers, ever weary of musket fire, Mattie and Devil came upon the farm buildings past the entrenchments of the British. This was the beginning outpost of Hougoumont. They were moving from the direction of the orchard towards the rear facing kitchen gardens of the farmhouses when battle cries alerted him not to go any further as the French were attacking the external gardens and north gate. Looking along the farm wall Mattie could see that parts of it had been blown away and spurring on his trusty steed, jumped into an area where the British were providing the sternest resistance.

"That was some jump," said a solider of the Coldsteam Guards, who brought Devil to a standstill for Mattie by grabbing his bridle. Mattie asked where MacDonnell could be found and was ushered to a partly standing farm out-building. The fighting, much of it hand to hand, raged all around but on making it to the British command post, Mattie panted out: "Sir, I come from Wellington himself with an express message for you." Mattie breathlessly relayed the epistle word for word and the Colonel's stern visage broke a wry smile that seemed completely out of place given the gunfire and screams emanating from just a few yards away.

"My lad, if only you could go back whence you came, I would gladly send the message back to the Duke saying that I have no choice but to comply with his orders. We have just been completely surrounded as you see. My troops are about to be overrun at any second. 'The end' up to which the Duke mentioned he wanted us to fight, is now almost at hand and I do not know how to rally the last of my men any more than I already have. Take your place, Officer, wheresoever you are best placed and prepare to die fighting."

Mattie turned to look for a place to make his stand, thinking only now of the pigeon concealed within Devil's saddlebags and how his mission for the Doctor would be left undone. No matter though, Mattie was a keen fighter and where there was a will, there was a way. If it were God's will, that pigeon would carry its message by the end of today.

These thoughts soon disappeared without trace when a sudden cry lifted from the front lines of the men he reluctantly joined. "They're through the main gate and into the farm!" As the throng of French uniforms flooded towards their group, Mattie spotted the enormous frame of an axe-wielding Frenchman. Mattie could not stand by, now anxiously watching as this gargantuan Franc was heading ominously in the direction of Devil. Mattie's only thought was for the safekeeping of his horse and Doctor Darwin's all-important pigeon nestled snugly in the saddlebags.

Mattie ignored the commanding officer's orders of holding the line and freely charged from his place among the British men. As he flew into the open fray of battle he aimed himself correctly in the direction of the axe-wielding Frenchman. Drawing nearer he took his stance, unsheathed his sabre and with a single precise blow Mattie decapitated the huge French marauder. The sickening crunch of a severed neck echoed over the grounds of the farmland and fell upon the taut ears of the British. Now out in the open on his own and vulnerable away from his fellow soldiers, Mattie had little choice but to then set about the other French troops who had followed their leader. Some he managed to dispatch just as easy as the now headless giant, while the other younger and more fearful Francs scattered in panic and disarray.

Mattie struggled with his steed and eventually led Devil to a safer berth. As he settled his horse with calming whispers, he heard a Frenchman cry out "Our Enforcer is dead!"

At that moment, the French who had made it through the gate halted and began to pull back. Buoyed by the sight and sounds of Mattie's achievements, the British troops charged with newly found vigour. Screaming proudly they drove the French into retreat. Back through the plundered gates they went, where their demoralised force could now be heard shouting the news of the fallen leader, killed by Mattie's own hand, "Legos has been beheaded, retreat!" Unknown to Mattie and all not part of the

French Battalion, Legos was Devil's recently dispatched would-be assassin and had once been the great French hero at Borodino where he had single-handedly forced the Russian troops onto the defensive. On account of his unrivalled bravery and strength, he had been the leader of the Hougoumont assault and without him, they had lost any edge they once held over the British. With his loss came a lack of French morale so severe that the tide truly turned in the British favour that day, in that battle, and Hougoumont stayed safe.

Mattie did not hear anything after the cry of French retreat and the huzzah of British victory as while he tended to Devil a single blow of shrapnel caught him on the side of his head, toppling him to his knees, although he still managed to keep a clutch on his horse and valuable cargo. The soldiers, upon witnessing his injury, rushed over to where Mattie was struggling, finding the area surrounding him strewn with the bodies of half a dozen dead or wounded French soldiers. They pried his hand free of Devil's bridle, ignoring his moans and carried him to the safety of their temporary field hospital housed in a barn.

The army surgeon treated Mattie's wounds and left him to rest, his head and left eye swaddled in bandages. After a short while Mattie came around, wracked with pain in his arm, leg and not least his head. Despite the agony of his wounds, the very thought of failing Doctor Darwin compelled him to attempt to find his way back to the Headquarters of General Hill. It was upon this man's final word of the battle's outcome that Mattie had been instructed to release the bird.

He staggered out of the makeshift hospital and inquired of a few soldiers where his jet-black steed had been tied. Fretfully he was told it had been taken to the back of the farmhouse to protect it from the French who were still fighting hard to storm and capture Hougoumont. Mattie stumbled across the farmyard to great acclaim from the British soldiers and was continually clapped on the back while being helped to mount his horse.

Mattie asked, "Which is the best way back to Headquarters?" and was directed through the orchard, as control of that area had recently been won back from the French. With no easing of his pains and little sense of direction the hero of the hour set out to find the British high command and release his hidden cargo.

Mattie had not travelled far when he heard some shouting emerging from the surrounding smoke. By this point in the battle, Wellington had formed his troops into approximately twenty squares or oblongs in two rows, in what could be likened to a chequer board pattern. The square was the classic formation to resist cavalry, as horses could not be enticed to charge into tightly formed squares bristling with bayonets. In front of these squares Wellington had deployed eleven artillery batteries comprising of Howitzers and six and nine pound guns. The gunners were under strict instructions not to discharge their arms until the French cavalry were virtually upon them. They were then to abandon their overweight weaponry and retreat to take refuge inside the squares.

As Mattie avoided the bloodshed wherever he could, as he came steadily closer to the British lines there was a massive formation of troops assembled in the 'form square' position.

As Mattie rode even closer to the bristling wall of men he was greeted with a shout:

"What mob you from, then?"

"Fifteenth Hussars," he managed to call back. Immediately the square parted, allowing him and Devil to make their way through. Mattie looked around and estimated a British force of roughly two thousand men plus horses and canons. As he navigated the endless troops awaiting the battle-line, he asked of a Sergeant the latest update of battle news and was informed: "The Frenchies cavalrymen are trying to outflank us and we have taken the square formation to stop the blighters in their tracks!"

Mattie took Devil to the centre of the square and tethered him to a string of other horses, but also took a moment to check the pigeon was safe. He discovered the bird was trembling with fear and could only hope it would last the day. The image of Doctor Darwin standing beside Devil entered Mattie's thoughts but for a second and he suddenly drifted further and further away as indeed did everything else. He had become faint-headed thanks to his recent injuries. He felt his body collapse from within and as all went dark, Mattie heard a timid "coo-coo" from the saddlebags above him.

By the time Mattie came to, a soldier sat alongside and was giving him water. The sun had risen further into the sky and the cloudy panorama above was at its brightest. There was a hum of chatter in the vicinity but it was sometime before Mattie could make out specific words. When he did, 'brave' 'bravery' and 'hero' were the ones he heard most often.

"What time is it?" he asked in a frail voice that sounded no more improved when he further enquired, "and how is the battle going?"

"You are going to have to ask the officer in charge, young Sir. I'm sure he will oblige such a brave fellow as you," said the orderly attending him. As he attempted to lift himself up onto his elbows an officer appeared at his side. Mattie repeated his enquiry regarding the state of the battle. The Officer leaned forward to explain the good news of how the Prussians had come into the foray and how the French were now in full retreat, even including their elite guard. "But I need to know one thing from you," said the Sergeant, "Are you Private Matthews?"

Mattie scrutinised the Sergeant for a brief second and confirmed this with a nod of his head.

"A message has come from General Hill that you are to return to him at once. He believed you were at Hougoumont." Mattie knew full well that he was needed elsewhere and needed to press on if he was to complete his arduous task.

Climbing stiffly onto Devil, thanks to the major assistance from the men surrounding him, Mattie jeered Devil to a steady gallop in the direction of the Duke Wellington's Headquarters with the men cheering to see him off.

When he finally arrived at Headquarters, having steered as clear of gunfire and brawling as possible, Mattie asked for an audience with General Hill, only to be told he had gone and was still out in the field. The officers demanded that Mattie remain until the Commander returned. Since the considerable pain from his wounds was becoming harder and harder to bear, Mattie agreed asking for a place where he could rest. He was shown to a stable where he just managed to secure Devil before collapsing exhausted onto a pile of hay.

It was dark by the time Mattie awoke and the weak candle light revealed a Doctor treating his wounds, going to and from his bedside in the now blanket covered hay. Mattie asked how the battle had gone and was happily told the French had now been completely routed.

With a resigned smile, the Doctor said, "Lad, with wounds such as yours, I think you should be thinking of other things", and then paused briefly saying, "like preparing for your last moments."

In spite of the intense pain, Mattie decided that waiting for General Hill was not an option open to him and to the Doctor's great surprise, he staggered to his feet and lurched over to Devil. Mattie took the bird from the saddlebags and carried it with all the care he could muster to the door. He threw the pigeon into the air where it fluttered into the night sky, high above the victorious battleground before turning for home.

"Job done," he said meekly, before collapsing into a heap and falling unconscious once again.

ELEVEN

Bertie Returns

After a day of fitful sleep, containing many ups and downs and the most unkind of loud noises, Bertie found himself unceremoniously pulled from the saddle pouch. Having been in darkness for hours he blinked into the light where he found himself in Mattie's hands but he could tell instantly, due to the congealing blood on the young man's hands and face that Mattie had been party to much bloodshed this day. Bertie could feel the shivers of pain going through Mattie's body as he placed a piece of paper into the container on his leg before the wounded hero turned Bertie loose to take flight.

As he climbed into the night's sky, Bertie surveyed the scene of devastation below: the battlefield was lit by flames that cast onto debris strewn over the vast area. With darkness rapidly descending he wondered why humans went to such lengths to inflict such pain on one another. He remembered hearing Doctor Darwin talk of "Man's blind indifference to his fellow man," when referring to war, an act that a man dedicated to saving lives could never comprehend, let alone this humble messenger pigeon.

Beneath him the carnage was still evident even as he traversed the black sky. Not only were dead human bodies stacked in ungainly piles, Bertie was also aghast to see the amount of dead horses littered across this scene of devastation. He felt sad observing the cruelty men had reeked upon man's hardest working friend in the animal world and asked himself how men could do this to creatures they loved and so depended upon? The corpses of these magnificent beasts presented a most sickening sight and now they would be left to the indulgence of carrion crows. After what men were calling the greatest battle in the history of Europe, there would be victory parades with horses in pride of place, but the ones lying dead or dying below had only known fear and suffering.

As he approached the perimeter of the battlefield, Bertie noticed a mass of people he did not recognise, not dressed in any military uniform, but he realised they were only there to begin stripping the dead.

On the wind he heard a cry of, "Look, there's a pigeon! Shoot!" He took this to mean it was time to wing his way fast and far from this wretched place, and as he did so Bertie thought indignantly, "Have they not had enough killing for one day?"

Flying over woods and fields he thought of the delights promised to him by the Doctor upon his return. There would be a long-awaited reunion with Hettie which already provided an extra boost to his flight, but the Doctor's extra promise of a well-earned retirement would have been an attractive proposition by itself, even if he had not added with a wink that he would also ensure as many hens as Bertie could possibly manage.

After many indulgent thoughts of the winnings to come his way, far below Bertie now lay a coastline he recognised. A vast stretch of water ending at white cliffs extended beneath him. Bertie had made this journey many times and knew that by this point, home was not too far away. Often while traversing the sea he had rested or slept on the mast of a passing ship, but all along he knew his return was eagerly awaited so carried on relentlessly towards his destination. Bertie knew it was an important task that Doctor Darwin had asked Mattie and he to carry out, so he swept on to ensure the good Doctor was not left disappointed. When he reached London, his final destination, Bertie knew Hettie was only moments away but it was the Doctor who was awaiting his arrival when he came to land in the loft of the rented address.

Doctor Darwin held Bertie close to his chest and gently removed the paper from the container on his leg. Patiently he unravelled it and after a brief glimpse at the message contained therein, let out a great shout, "Eureka!"

When the Doctor placed him into the loft where he found his lovely Hettie waiting, Bertie also shouted an indecipherable, but equally excited, "Eureka!"

TWELVE

Money Laced With Treason
Friday 16th June - Mon 19th June 1815

The Doctor watched proceedings at the stock exchange with a smile as the men from Shrewsbury entered the building. Each one gave the impression of being drunk and they had begun staggering around from trader to trader, asking how to buy shares and make a fortune.

On this morning of Friday 16th June, the market was nervous and jumpy due to the impending battle soon to take place somewhere in Belgium. There was obvious anxiety about the outcome but most were, outwardly at least, confident that Wellington would defeat Napoleon, thus ensuring peace would return to Europe and with it a healthy and prosperous economy.

This uncouth group of farmers, all making a nuisance of themselves, were looked upon with much disdain. But the sharpest traders could smell a profit at the expense of these drunken bumpkins and as the saying went, "A fool and his money is easy parted."

The first to trade was Thomas Eyton who was trying hard not to give away his accent, while also creating much mirth among his companions. News soon spread through the Stock Exchange about how these men had made fortunes from the war and were willing to buy shares in practically anything, if the price seemed right and the chat sound. In due course, some traders sold the dysfunctional group bankrupted shares and this turned to the great delight of other colleagues who were very eager to sell off their useless stock to these country oafs. The endearing factor for such quick sales was that this loutish group only made payment with readily accepted cash and bankers' notes. Quite a crowd gathered around the Doctor's party, some amused, some disgusted by their antics but at close of business that day a number of traders were showing a very healthy profit and were equally greatly enthused by the prospect of this ragamuffin group returning the following week.

That evening at The Swan, the Masons met in a room guarded by Mark Briggs, Doctor Darwin's coachman. The Doctor started by congratulating them on their performance in the Stock Exchange and reiterated that when they returned there again on Monday, the impression must once again be that of innocents inviting exploitation. He reinforced the notion of feigning drunkenness but was at his most emphatic when he stressed there was to be no actual drinking amongst them. When they did return in forty hours time, on his command they were to purchase any and all Government consuls that traders would surely rush to sell them. For this they required a substantial amount in bankers' draughts, which the Doctor was covering, allowing them to spend a fortune on apparently useless consuls.

When the Stock Market opened on the morning of Monday 19th June, trading opened in a jittery manner as traders waited nervously for news of the battle's imminent outcome. The big guns of the trading fraternity were observed more closely than usual to detect whether they had any inkling of how the battle had gone. Correct information reaching a speculator could be worth millions.

The market had only been open a few minutes when the Shrewsbury group entered but their arrival was barely noticed against the backdrop of nervousness that shrouded proceedings. It was not long however before the intensity increased further when rumours that Napoleon had defeated both Wellington and the Prussians began to spread like wildfire, fuelled predominantly by the fact that Doctor Darwin and Nathan Rothschild were dumping consuls in an unseen panic. This suggested to the traders that two conspirators had been alerted to a British defeat at Waterloo. The trading in consuls dived from seventeen shillings and continued falling until they reached nearly rock bottom and rested at the unheard of price of 'tuppence a share'.

This was the moment Doctor Darwin had been waiting for. He gave the subtle hand signal to his fellow Masons to start buying, in order to divert the real dealers. They bought slowly and slobbishly at first with no fixed pattern to avoid suspicion and all the while still maintaining the pretence of being drunk.

The traders were only too happy to sell their consuls at this nominal price, completing another successful stage of the plot.

One trader realised this was the same group of buffoons who

had caused amusement a few days earlier and was heard to remark: "That bunch of arseholes from Shropshire is at it again."

As the day wore on, there was no shortage of traders prepared to sell them stock that was evidently worthless due to the suspected defeat of Britain.

The stock market was in absolute chaos but to the cool head the reward for this contest was sure to be unimaginable wealth.

That evening, with the Shropshire Masons safely ensconced back at The Swan, Doctor Darwin spoke to the group one last time before curfew.

"Gentlemen, today you have done yourselves and Shrewsbury proud. You must now return to your homes as soon as possible before anyone realises your true purpose and identity. God forbid anyone should hazard a guess that you were working for me and our secret banker."

While the Stock Exchange had been duped by the Doctor's master plan, the outlying members of the Shropshire cast were, in turn, unaware of their role in creating a diversionary action which had allowed the two leading men, Darwin and Rothschild, to buy vast amounts of consuls at ridiculously low prices. It was all down to the strength of knowing the outcome of the biggest battle in the history of England. Doctor Darwin's team had fooled many powerful men in their adventure, men who would surely reap their revenge if ever they found out. The most powerful of these men was the King and his revenge would certainly end with a short sharp snap at the base of a man's neck.

THIRTEEN

The Rewards Are Worth The Trouble
25ᵗʰ June 1815

The Old House Inn, located on the Shrewsbury thoroughfare known as Dogpole, had hosted many gatherings of the great and the not so good. The short-term residents had ranged from those on the wrong side of the law, to Priests in hiding and even a Queen (Mary Tudor, later Queen Mary) awaiting her arrest. But those assembled in the Old House's drawing room sat under a canvas of the Tudor Rose, Crown and the Pomegranate on the evening of June 25ᵗʰ 1815 were there for only one reason; to collect their personal share of a business deal that generated more money than any other in Shrewsbury's long history.

Each man was aware of the risk he had taken by committing himself to such a plot and accepted the penalty if ever their deeds were uncovered as 'death by hanging', leaving behind families both disgraced and bankrupt.

The Doctor spoke quietly but with confidence when he told them everything was now dependent upon their silence and care when handling the huge sum of money they would shortly be receiving. He stressed they were now bound together by mutual dependency and there was not another sound to be heard as the Doctor began revealing to his cohorts the full nature of their triumph.

"Gentlemen, I would like to thank you for the wonderful operation you carried out last week," to which one or two nodded acknowledgement, "and I will now lay out your rewards." There was a cough or wheeze from a couple of them to disguise their nervousness but the room had fallen quiet once more when Doctor Darwin resumed speaking.

"Firstly you will all receive one thousand pounds in gold within the week. Secondly a one hundred pounds deposit of gold will be sent to your accounts every six months for five years." Out of respect to the Doctor there was no audible response. However, the smiles around the room were wide and uncontained. "Thirdly, at the end of this time, if you have followed the rules of silence and moderate living, all will be revealed to you of where I have invested the remainder on your behalf. But I assure gentlemen, you will be wealthy for the rest of your lives."

He continued, "What I have arranged we shall refer to from here on in as 'The fund' and it is twofold. Nobody must have knowledge of your investments. If anyone were to leak this knowledge to any authority, an inquiry will surely take place into events that occurred during that fateful day on the money markets and all our necks would surely feel the pinch. Just remember, there are always jealous men, those who will use the law to get at this money. They will do all they can and no doubt violence would surely be part of their inquiry. So long as you stick to the oath you have taken, the future looks bright and for many years we can keep meeting through our mother lodge without raising concern. Of course, should any of you fine gentlemen ever require an ear sooner than our regular meets, I can visit you all as your doctor without anyone being the wiser."

Noting their relaxed, self-satisfied expressions, Doctor Darwin chose this moment to propel a note of caution into the rarefied air of expectant prosperity.

"I'm sure that you all know or have heard tell of a woman named Catherine Plymley. When I said that nobody must know of these matters, this of course includes even your wives. I am certain that this Plymley woman is a cohort to every word of gossip in Shropshire." His voice was now firm and without a hint of compromise. "The woman of whom I speak is the greatest danger to us. If a word were to slip from one of your wives to her our secrecy would be in jeopardy. Her own brother, let me remind you, is a high-ranking tax official. The fact of which, I am sure has already crossed the mind of Thomas Eyton here," Eyton solemnly nodded in agreement, "since he, as you know, is collector of taxes for all Shropshire."

Doctor Darwin re-adjusted his stance once more to take in the entire room.

"Gentlemen, a loose tongue at any time can lead to disaster for us all." At which each and every man in the room expressed total agreement by conferring with one and other and reiterating their commitment to their agreed silence.

As the mumbling grew louder, the Doctor intervened, "I must tell you that there are other partners in this venture and from it they too have made significant sums of money. Nonetheless, these are powerful, ruthless men, who will stop at nothing to maintain their good names and of course their money. I assure you all, they will stretch as far as to murder for it if needed."

Given the grave news, there were far fewer smiling faces now. Some in fact were unable to hide their apprehension so he offered the following words of reassurance, "Gentlemen, all you have to do is live within your means and keep your oath. Do those two things and all will be well for evermore. Pray though and never fail to bear in mind that above all things, alcohol can loosen a tongue."

For the first time in the entire evening, one of audience chose to respond. Doctor Darwin was interrupted by John Rocke, in whose home the meeting was taking place. Indeed, The Old House had been in his family for many generations.

"My dear Doctor," Darwin along with everybody else in the room turned to look at Rocke, who seemed unaffected by the sudden attention. "You always go on about our drinking, but a servant of mine, whom you recommended to me from your very own household, told me that every night before you go to bed Evans brings you a glass of gin and a carafe of water for dilution."

If his intention had been to bring some levity to the occasion, then Rocke failed miserably as the others sat stony faced, taking a cue from their leader, who was clearly quite annoyed.

"If the nosey servant was more observant he would have noticed the so-called gin is in fact boiling water," said the Doctor bristling with irritation, "and the carafe is to cool the boiling water. Most of you gentlemen know I recommend that you always go to bed with hot water as your last drink of the day." As humorous a retort as it may have been in the right situation, the Doctor held a bitter gaze on Mr Rocke without even a hint of smiling. Shortly after that the meeting was brought to a close.

As Doctor Darwin's coach rumbled over the cobbled streets of Shrewsbury back to Mount House, he reflected upon the success of his mission which it was fair to claim had made him possibly the richest man in England. If he had a concern that evening it was solely for the whereabouts of Mattie, his eventful emissary. The Doctor consoled himself that soon enough the young man would arrive home safely and in good health.

Way up in a cloudless, navy blue sky stars twinkled and shone and when a warm peaceful breeze ruffled a tree here and there, a perfect summer evening was complete.

Shrewsbury, he concluded in that instant was a wonderful place to be. He signalled to Mark Briggs, his burly coachman, to follow behind with the coach as he had decided to walk awhile. The Doctor walked from the furthermost point of Dogpole down into Ox Lane, but happenstance had not taken him this way. He chose this route in order to see the little house he had bought for Mattie and Alice earlier that week.

On the opposite side of the road outside the ancient church of St Mary's, he spotted the parish beadle Mr Wycherley out and about. As they passed by they offered each other a "Goodnight" greeting. One of the many roles in the church life of the beadle was to escort unmarried pregnant women, who were not of the parish, to adjoining areas. This would then prevent any further costs of care to fall upon St Mary's, whose borders were defined by great stones around the centre of Shrewsbury. Over recent years the Doctor noted that many gentlemen had become accustomed to mount their horses using these very same stones. The beadle's practice was the church's underhand way of dealing with unmarried women, and the Doctor believed it to be inhuman and he never missed an opportunity of expressing this opinion to the 'good and holy' men of the cloth.

FOURTEEN

Return Of The Fallen Hussar
August 1815

Two months passed and August was well underway when Doctor Darwin finally heard news of Mattie. On that August morning he received a letter from General Hill which relayed the news that Mattie had been seriously wounded during the battle and following a period of convalescence would soon be returning to Shrewsbury. The date speculated upon by General Hill of Mattie's homecoming, given the slow rate of land post, was actually the very day of the letter's arrival, so without delay the Doctor instructed his butler that his coach was to be prepared immediately, as there was soon to be urgent business that would require his undivided attention.

As the Doctor boarded he gave a simple instruction to Mark, his coachman, "Take us straight round to old Mattie's house and don't spare the horses!"

When they arrived at Old Cruck House in Frankwell they were not the first to arrive and the place was already in an uproarious state, with neighbours gathered around the house cheering and waving flags.

The Doctor's first reaction was one of deep concern, fearing the crowd knew more than they should. This grew to a fear of his secret becoming the subject of speculation and rumour, but he then placated the worries by concluding any solider returning from such a momentous battle would receive such a reception as this. He instructed Mark to do the honours, namely testing the stairs to ensure they would take the Doctor's weight and when he had confirmation that they would, Doctor Darwin began his ascent.

Upon entering the room he instantly recognised the odour of rotting flesh, having been all too familiar with gangrene in his time. As he approached the bed, Mattie looked up but could barely recognise his visitor. Doctor Darwin quietly introduced himself and this information brought some recognition to Mattie's pale and crumpled face.

Through a haze of agony Mattie replied weakly, "Hello Doctor Darwin.....how are you? I....I did as you bid me," but this was all he could say before slipping back into his unconscious state.

Darwin went quickly to the top of the stairs shouting for his bag and once again a bowl of hot water. He told Mark to leave at once for Mount house and find the tin marked 'mould' stored on the highest of the shelves in his bureau, and then to return with all possible haste. With Mark gone in a flash and his orders being carried out, the Doctor stripped Mattie to ascertain the full extent of his injuries.

As he carefully removed the scant clothing he remarked, "Army Doctors do leave a lot to be desired in wound care," but mumbled promptly to himself, "I suppose with so many to treat they are still a Godsend to any wounded soldier." Not, of course, that Mattie was in any condition to join in the conversation.

By stripping Mattie the Doctor became aware of the nasty gash on the back of his head, the numerous cuts to his body, but worst of all was the deep laceration to his right leg, the likely result of a sword slash and the wound most affected by the gangrene.

He began to wash the wounds clean, noting the customary signs of the practise of 'bleeding' which prompted a brief, ironic smile as he wondered how they thought cutting a man to make him bleed would ever help a man already bleeding to death.

He heard Mark rush up the stairs, bursting into the bedroom flushed and panting, holding the tin in his outstretched gloved hand. When the Doctor opened it the smell in the room worsened even more, but he took a handful of the curious mould and rubbed it into the Mattie's wounds.

As he applied the awful smelling concoction he imagined a day when his fellow Doctors may understand the true power of this miraculous mould.

Darwin had come by it from his mentor and colleague Doctor Ling at Leyden University. Ling was firstly Doctor Darwin's friend and secondly a Chinaman who told him so many of the great medicinal secrets of ancient China. In his homeland Ling had studied under the great Chinese doctor, Wang Chin (Wang Qingen) and in turn furnished young Doctor Darwin with innovative treatments and often miraculous potions made from natural plants and mineral salts. Ling had never been slow to tell his colleague how long medicine had been a science in China, saying its study went back three thousand years. Doctor Darwin concluded at the time and was still of the opinion, that medical study in England was still in its infancy.

After administering what treatment he could, Doctor Darwin recommended that Mattie stay in bed and should be kept cool until the fever subsided. The Doctor also informed Alice of his intention to call everyday to monitor Mattie's condition. During the days that followed Mattie rarely regained consciousness and for the short periods he was awake, Alice took the opportunity to feed him. She was encouraged by how quickly the repugnant smell disappeared but her husband was still unable to remain awake for too long. After a fortnight the improvement in Mattie's health was apparent to everyone and gradually he began to sit up in bed and even speak a few words. He remembered nothing of Waterloo and his subsequent return to Shrewsbury but Doctor Darwin felt confident this was a reaction to all he had endured, assuring Alice that although memory loss could continue for some time Mattie would, at some point, regain the ability to recollect.

As Mattie's condition continued to improve, the opportunity arose for Doctor Darwin to tell Alice of the provision he had made for the couple. One morning, after his daily examination of Mattie had been conducted, he took Alice aside to speak with her.

"I would like you to move into a cottage on Ox Lane which I have purchased on your behalf. You have no need to wait as I have had it finished and newly furnished from top to bottom. It has a good fire and fresh water from a deep well. Also, I have opened an account with the person from whom I receive my meat and vegetables on your behalf. You will not be charged for anything, as Mattie must be fed the very best food available. I will send someone everyday to make sure everything is fine and to nurse Mattie and clean for you. But you must still send for me at any time, day or night, if Mattie takes a turn for the worst. In between now and the point that he makes his full recovery, I will still make sure to call whenever I possibly can."

Darwin looked upon the battle scarred Mattie as if he were the crack through which an ill wind may blow. If indeed his full memory returned and he began to recall the favour he carried out for the Doctor, there was the obvious threat of Doctor Darwin and his cohorts being compromised. Not that the Doctor ever questioned young Mattie's loyalty, but he knew that the damage to Mattie's mind could be worse than just his memory. It would be particularly concerning if anyone from the Government or military should begin asking him questions. The Doctor resolved to prevent any such eventuality and stressed to Alice the paramount need for Mattie to have complete peace and quiet in which to convalesce.

The Doctor had far from forgotten the threat posed by an unwanted enquiry closer to home, in the form of diarist and ever-present busybody Catherine Plymley. In the past the mere mention of her name was enough to make the Doctor's blood run cold. Since the Waterloo escapade he had to be more guarded against her inquiries than ever before. Combining her thirst for gossip with her notorious vocation and the addition of the lofty position held by her brother in the treasury, the merest hint of scandal could be enough for the cards to start tumbling. Last but not least, there was also the added worry of her brother being in regular contact with Thomas Eyton in his position of Inspector of Taxes for Shropshire. With new income tax legislation imminent, there was even more likelihood of dialogue between the two men which gave grounds for concern in view of ongoing speculation concerning Eyton's lavish outgoings and public funds. Needless to say, even with the treasonous deed done, the Doctor had more qualms than ever.

The rumours of Eyton's excesses had reached the Doctor's ears on more than one occasion over the last few weeks and he decided the time was fast approaching when Eyton would require some discreet advice on his spending habits and the responsibilities he had to his fellow Masons.

FIFTEEN

The Plot Nearly Boils Over
December 1815

Nearly six months had passed since the great battle and during this period a quiet and ever-growing satisfaction had taken root deep within the Doctor's mind. His life had settled into a pattern that brought no unwelcome intrusions. His fellow Masons for the most part had observed the guidelines Doctor Darwin had laid down with regard to their handsome windfall.

At the same time Mattie had displayed no obvious signs of fully remembering his deed for the Doctor. All in all, this gave Darwin good reason to believe the secret was well guarded, if not entirely safe. There was a small group of the Masons who had been unable to resist the temptation to spend, although nothing outlandish could be detected from Mr Rocke's recent purchase of some small local properties or Mr Loxdale's latest investment in a new house, as both were men of position and means. Doctor Darwin had also noted that Peele's wife was now sporting the finest gowns and hats but again it was not a matter for undue disquiet as she had been known to indulge in the occasional spree from time to time. The only one of whom it could be said was evidently indulging in highlife was, as Darwin had previously feared, Thomas Eyton. The new coach "King" that Eyton had purchased from a London manufacturer was an undisputed extravagance, but the Doctor remained hopeful that his lucrative salary as Shropshire's tax inspector would offset any suspicions about any acquisition of ulterior and improper wealth.

The Doctor decided to pay Mattie a call and set off on foot, telling his coachman to follow behind him closely. This was not an uncommon sight for the townsfolk of Shrewsbury. He crossed the Welsh Bridge and walked into Mardol before turning onto Pride

Hill. Just as he turned onto the rise a young street urchin appeared before him with a broom.

"Sweep the street for you sir?" called out the child who, before the Doctor could even say a word, began brushing the dirt from the Doctor's path to keep his shoes clean. The boy carried on a step ahead of Doctor Darwin until he had turned into Ox Lane and continued sweeping until the Doctor reached Mattie's front door. The Doctor reached into his pocket and offered the youngster a coin as reward, but payment was surprisingly refused by the young scamp.

"Apologies, Sir, but my mother would flay me alive for taking anything off the great Doctor, after what you does for us."

Wearing a bemused expression, Doctor Darwin replied, "This will be our secret then, a loan which you shall repay someday." The boy accepted the coin and a pat on the head for his efforts and skipped off toward whence he came.

Mattie was sitting up in bed and looked significantly improved than on his return from Waterloo, but he was still some way from a complete return to good health. Alice led the Doctor into the bedroom, where he greeted his patient with, "How are you feeling today, Mattie?"

Mattie moved his head and smiled as means of acknowledgment, offering the reply, "I'm just fine, Sir," in a fragile tone.

Alice whispered to Doctor Darwin that Mattie's memory was only showing the slightest signs of improvement. "I have to tell you though Doctor, last night a stranger called to visit saying he knew Mattie from the battle at Waterloo. I tried to discourage him from seeing Mattie, but he seemed so eager and I thought a visit from an old comrade may lift my Mattie's spirits. Mattie did seem to recognise him immediately. After the visitor had left though, I was ever so upset as Mattie became agitated and restless, hardly sleeping properly all night."

The Doctor reassured Alice that Mattie was fine but in fact it was now the turn of Doctor Darwin to feel agitated. "No one is to see or speak to Mattie unless I am in attendance from here on in. Do you understand me, Alice? I do not want any further disturbance to Mattie's recovery."

In reply to the Doctor's firm manner, Alice timidly agreed.

"If this man should call again, try to find out his name and business. I need to know whether he is a gentleman or as I suspect, just a thug from the battlefields. Give me your word Alice that under absolutely no circumstance are you to allow him to enter your home again." The good Doctor stifled his panic and bade Alice and Mattie farewell. As he made his way to the confines of his coach, sweat began to poor from his brow in distress.

All of a sudden, the carefree and comfortable existence of the past few months was under threat. The Doctor's trap-like mind swirled with nervous activity. Who was this unknown stranger and what did he want with Mattie? Was it a visit made in innocence or, and much more likely, did somebody want answers to some explanations to a catalogue of events in which the Doctor would be implicated at every turn. Doctor Darwin was a man not easily panicked but even he had deep-seated qualms at this recent development.

He knew it was now vital to speak with Thomas Eyton as the Doctor saw him as a source of danger that needed addressing without delay. Seizing the moment, he decided an immediate visit was imperative and shouted directions to his coachman Briggs.

Upon his arrival at Eyton's home there was no opportunity for careful and calculated dialogue as the Doctor found himself met with consternation. As he entered the home, servants conveyed that Thomas Eyton was in a dreadfully anxious state and close to a nervous breakdown. Darwin hurried into the drawing room to be at the side of his friend, whereupon Thomas Eyton explained the reason for his considerable disquiet. The Doctor was to hear a tale of embezzlement that sent a shiver down even his cast iron spine.

Eyton confessed to the Doctor that for some time now he had been taking money from the County's income tax account to set up his wife with a fortune. He had always hoped the Government would neither notice nor be able to recover it. The Doctor had sensed that his warning to the Masons about excessive spending may have been lost on Thomas Eyton and had intended for some time to reprimand him for his cavalier approach toward expenditure, but nothing prepared Darwin for the amount Eyton admitted to swindling. Eighteen thousand pounds was not a huge sum in relation to what the Stock Exchange episode had generated, but due to huge overspending his personal account was now in serious arrears and he had also siphoned off tax revenue into a separate account which he had fraudulently set up on his wife's behalf.

Inwardly the Doctor was seething that Eyton had been so reckless and greedy and knew in all likelihood the fraud would be discovered. That however was not an end to it. Worse news then followed from Eyton's lips. So staggered was Doctor Darwin when Eyton imparted his next bombshell that he had to reach for a chair in order to remain standing. Thomas had told the Commissioner of Taxes (Catherine Plymley's brother Joseph) that he could make up the deficit with money he could borrow from Doctor Darwin.

"I hope you can see your way to advance me some of the money from our little venture," Eyton asked hopefully. The Doctor said he would consider making a loan, but needed a little time to take stock.

In the early hours of the following morning, Doctor Darwin sat at his desk and after much evaluating decided to refuse Eyton's request for an advance loan. If he obliged the other Masons would be compromised and under no circumstances would he breach their agreed code for the disbursement of the bounty. Anything that might place his fellow Masons in danger must be avoided at all costs, so Eyton's plea for help simply had to be dismissed. With Christmas looming and the onset of a harsh winter, Darwin felt sure that the Government would not be undertaking any investigations at this time of year and would undoubtedly leave Eyton to boil in a stew of his own making. After all it was brought about by the man's own greed, attention-seeking pomp and crass complacency.

The Doctor rose from his desk and stood at the window watching the snowfall in thick dense flakes. As it fell and settled on the ground, he wished a Merry Christmas to one and all, even the foolhardy Thomas Eyton.

When Christmas arrived, it found the Doctor and the Darwin household to be in a general state of happiness and contentment. Doctor Darwin had an increasing feeling of security as the festive season gave way to the early weeks of January 1816, buoyed by the fact there had been no further scares concerning either Mattie or Thomas Eyton. Being the time of year for resolutions, he now felt in a position to fulfil his long-held ambition of being the biggest private money lender in the country.

All the Yuletide cheer and salutation swiftly began to evaporate like melting snow, when Darwin received word in early February that Eyton needed to meet with him on a matter of utmost urgency.

Noon was approaching that day just as Doctor Darwin entered the house, to be greeted with tidings of distress, where Thomas, said to be inconsolable, had issued strict instructions that only the Doctor was to be allowed access to him. Darwin hurried to the drawing room in which Eyton had taken refuge, finding his accomplice in a dark and sombre mood. He lay on the chaise longue, a frightened man with visions of damnation before his eyes. Thomas revealed that Joseph Plymley had dismissed all offers of repayment, with the Government intent on making an example of how embezzlers were to be dealt with, serving notice on Eyton that criminal proceedings against him would be forthcoming. Left in no doubt that his name would go forward for prosecution, Eyton trembled as he spoke, his face red and contorted.

As a precaution the Doctor administered a potion to this deeply troubled man, which took Eyton into a peaceful sleep. With him quietened Darwin used the time to think of how this dilemma could be solved, but when Thomas awoke Darwin had not been able to fully formulate a resolution to the issue.

When Thomas had come round sufficiently to comprehend what the Doctor had to say, he heard Darwin state, "I think this refusal is only a threat and eventually they will back down and offer a compromise." Choosing his words carefully, the Doctor continued that, "Taking any of the remaining money back from your wife and repaying the Government immediately may result in the desired effect," and was the only course of action to take.

Eyton thanked the Doctor for his advice and by the time Darwin departed, appeared to be a lot less burdened.

Later that evening, as the Doctor was later informed, Eyton had taken to his office leaving the express wish of "not to be disturbed." Sometime in the hours that followed, Thomas Eyton resolved to take his own life and did so by shooting himself in the mouth, forcing the lead ball down his throat and rupturing a main artery. Having fallen silent in his bureau for some time, his ever-diligent house-servants followed his strict instructions of not disturbing him, but out of sheer concern called upon the Doctor once more to return.

Eyton had left a letter for Doctor Darwin, confessing that there was no money in his wife's account with which to recompense the Government and that every penny he had dishonestly obtained had been spent. Believing a conviction to be imminent, he had no desire to place his fellow Masons in a vulnerable position, so concluded there was no alternative other than to take his own life.

At that moment, sharing a closed office with the corpse of an old colleague, Doctor Darwin saw an honourable strength in Eyton that he had not previously recognised. But there was little time to acknowledge chivalry no matter how noble, as Darwin needed to explain Eyton's demise to the household.

Nobody had actually heard the fatal shot as Thomas still had the presence of mind to wrap the small gun in a thick cloth which cloaked the sound, leaving a dull thud as the only noise to be heard, one that sounded like someone falling to the floor.

Given the internal course of Eyton's bullet, and lack of exit wound; the Doctor solemnly informed Eyton's next of kin that Thomas had become so emotionally enraged that he had caused a blood vessel in his throat to rupture and as a result had fainted and bled to death.

Darwin asked for water and cloths so he could begin cleaning up the pool of blood, but offered not the slightest suggestion that Thomas had taken his own life.

The Doctor knew desperate men used this method of committing suicide - shooting themselves in the mouth with a small pistol which left no signs of violence to the body, only a burn to the face which could be cleaned and hidden with make-up. In the event of a businessman resorting to such a tragic measure, the body of the deceased had to be displayed so that his creditors could see neither suicide nor foul play was the cause of death and helped convince them that their money was not in jeopardy.

The next morning, after Doctor Darwin had spent most of the previous night in the role of mortician and applying the necessary powders and potions to disguise the truth, the body was laid out on a table in the front room of the Eyton's house. The servants had been the first to view the late Thomas Eyton, primarily as a means of spreading the news far and wide that he had died of natural causes. Such a conclusion would ensure that tax collectors could not collect on the debt of a dead man and also keep the full extent of Eyton's dishonesty hidden; only ever revealed to Darwin in his parting letter which the Doctor had moved quickly to conceal.

For the Doctor, there was now the urgent matter of retrieving the money he had invested in the same bank Eyton had defrauded, as banks were frequently collapsing after a large lender defaulted on a loan.

He told coachman Briggs that he needed to visit the Old Bank of Shrewsbury with the utmost urgency and arrived to seek a private audience with the manager. Darwin explained that due to a large and unexpected bill he needed to empty his account immediately, but would return the following day with funds to keep the account open. Twenty-four hours later, however, the bank was closed 'until further notice', once the news of Eyton's debt became common knowledge, which in itself had sent shockwaves throughout Shrewsbury and its banks. The Old Bank of Shrewsbury immediately stopped payments as they quickly realised the scale of Eyton's liabilities. Three other Shrewsbury banks came under pressure to pay out and a run started on them. People thronged the streets as if a fair were in town. One of the banks, Rowtons, was completely bankrupted as a consequence of the recent calamity. Two others sent partners to London in a bid to raise support and only after securing sufficient funds were they able to answer the demands placed upon them. The Old Bank of Shrewsbury remained closed for almost two weeks. When it did reopen, Doctor Darwin felt empowered enough to feel the worst of the crisis had been withstood, for now at least.

Despite feeling more content as the episode slipped into the past, the Doctor would bide his time before telling Eyton's widow of the substantial inheritance due to her. For the moment it suited his purpose that she be perceived insolvent.

SIXTEEN

The Heat Is On

The pattern of a month's turmoil followed by six months of relative serenity continued for the Doctor, but another period of quiet ended with a message from Mattie requesting an urgent meeting.

Doctor Darwin was greeted by Alice whose troubled expression right away suggested danger. There had been a return visit by the stranger who had called on them last December, only this time Alice told him that Mattie could only have non-family visitors in the presence of his Doctor upon whose authority the decision had been taken for the good of the patient.

When informed of this, the stranger became rude and gave an air of threat, but nevertheless Alice stood her ground, took his name and learned that he was staying at The Raven Hotel. She informed him that if the Doctor thought it wise, she would contact him again and arrange for him to speak with Mattie, but only with Doctor Darwin in attendance.

The man had been called Stanger and she described him to the Doctor as standing over six feet tall, of muscular build with black hair and dark scary eyes. His voice was rough and he wore a scarf that partially hid a deep scar on his neck. After he left, she ascended the stairs and found Mattie out of bed, coiled in fear as he recognised the man's voice as that of 'The Killer of Hougoumont.' When she had settled him back into his bed again, Alice questioned him once more about the reason for his panic. All Mattie did was curl up in a state of shock and kept repeating "Hougoumont killer" over and over before slipping back into a fitful sleep.

Darwin thought it best for all parties if he saw Mattie alone and so Alice went for a walk while they talked. When she had departed, the Doctor took a small bottle from his bag and told Mattie, who was barely awake, to swallow the contents of the cup offered to him. The liquid had a rapid impact as within five minutes Mattie emerged from his stupor to offer a precise answer to the Doctor's question, as to just who this 'Killer of Hougoumont' was.

Mattie thought for a mere moment and then spoke with more clarity than at any time since his return from the pivotal battle of Waterloo.

"Doctor, he was the man in charge of interrogating captured French prisoners at Hougoumont. We all presumed that the screaming we kept hearing was coming from soldiers dying in the battle, but later on, just before the French broke in, I found the true source of the torment we heard. I was on my way to secure Devil when I went past the furthest barn where the prisoners were kept under guard and I saw disrobed bodies lying outside in a heap; they had all been badly mauled and mutilated. When I asked the guard on duty about this morbid sight, I was told not to ask as "it was the work of Stanger". The guard then told me to help him get the corpses thrown over the wall where the French who died in the farmyard skirmish had been dumped."

Mattie moved his head and looked toward the window as if he sought the strength to continue. "This Stanger is an evil man who worked on behalf of the secret agents of Wellington. God knows that Wellington could not have been aware of what methods this monster used in order to get his information."

With this remark, the drug began to wear off and Mattie's eyes glazed over; he grew silent once more and began to lie back in bed. Darwin issued a silent word of thanks to Doctor Ling whose potion, the one Mattie had just imbibed, had on many occasions proved to bring patients back from the brink of unconsciousness. When they did return, no matter how briefly, they could never tell a lie. The Doctor knew that he must meet this man, Stanger, even if only to ascertain his motive for being in Shrewsbury.

When Alice returned she was told Mattie was tired but in a comfortable state and the Doctor said he would return later for a final check before nightfall. Darwin went back to his coach and told Mark he would be making the short walk to The Raven Hotel, but as was customary, Mark was to follow closely behind and when he had parked the coach was to find the Doctor in the Hotel parlour. The coachman was not to acknowledge the Doctor but to sit in a chair with its back to Doctor Darwin and his acquaintance.

There was no mistaking Stanger when he entered the room. He met Alice's description perfectly, however the Doctor would have gone as far as to describe his overall demeanour as pure evil and absolutely dangerous. He found it incredible that Alice could have even stood in the same room as this man, let alone face him down on a doorstep. Darwin, somewhat nervously, walked up to the "killer" and introduced himself, saying Mattie Matthews was his patient. Not one to be indirect, the Doctor asked Stanger what business he had with this very sick man.

When the Doctor sat down Stanger responded to the question, his replies bristling with sharpness.

"Why Doctor, I have been empowered by the Government, after serving many years in good service in the War Department catching spies and traitors. I am here today to uncover a sinister plot Sir, one which goes against our King and Country. A group has managed to undermine His Majesty's Government by making a strong attempt at destabilizing our fragile economy, all for the good of the French and that bastard Napoleon."

Although outwardly aggressive and brutish, Stanger conversed in a forthright and confident manner and Darwin quickly concluded this was a man not to be taken lightly. Stanger continued:

"God was on our side that day and victory was ours in France. The Government have since decided that the home-bound assault on our economy has to be exposed even if only to deter others and they aim to set an example of this treasonous team by means of the gallows."

Doctor Darwin drew a deep breath and coughed, giving him a few extra seconds to consider a reply. "But what can a mere solider of the ranks have to do with such an intricate plot? This young man is a noble lad, I have known him all of his life."

"I have discovered eye witness reports that this "noble lad", your patient Matthews, was seen releasing a pigeon from the battlefield of Waterloo. Apparently he was heavily wounded, but made this release just after the outcome had been decided. We have reason to believe he was more than likely sending the news of victory to England, so that these treasonous enemies could take advantage of our Government's economy, all for profit. Needless to say, it was at the expense of our Royal Majesty." Stanger raised a fingertip to his eyebrow in a curious salute. "Given this information I have more than enough reason to believe that Matthews would obviously be in a position to identify the person or persons involved. I assure you Doctor, that by fair or foul means I am fully authorised to uncover the culprits and bring them to justice."

"And you carry the credentials of this authority about your person?" said the Doctor, being careful not to goad Stanger into a loss of temper.

"I do, good Doctor. I have it safe in my pocket along with a list of names of those suspected of being involved in the nefarious deed. Your Mattie is just the top of the list." Darwin took a moment to absorb this revelation. "Doctor," Stanger continued, in a voice of controlled severity and cruelty, "I do not require your permission to see Matthews as the warrant I carry gives me full powers of arrest. Until now, I have merely been polite. I have made enquiries in Shrewsbury and found you to be a man beyond reproach, a God fearing citizen who is loyal to the King. Given your reputation, I demand a moment to talk to Matthews once more before I leave. I ask that it be certainly no later than the day after tomorrow. This would even give me a little time to taste the delights of Shrewsbury." With a gesture completely out of character, Stanger gave the Doctor a sly wink, bade him goodnight and, as a parting comment, said he would wait a day for his request to be honoured.

The Doctor's mind was ablaze with connotations. He expected the oath taken by the Masons to withstand any amount of interrogation, but Mattie was the imponderable and if he cracked under Stanger's intensive questioning Darwin would be left in a defenceless position where not even his upstanding reputation could save him.

The next morning the Doctor rose early and asked Mark to drive him to a low part of Shrewsbury, notorious for its criminal fraternity. His presence at the Elephant & Castle public house in Mardol (meaning 'the street of the devil') was not altogether unusual as for many years the landlady, Nellie Davies, had been one of his patients. Her medical problems stemmed from a love of bare fist fighting which took place just a short distance away in The Quarry. On more than one occasion large crowds of both men and women gathered to watch Nellie fight. Such was her pugilistic prowess that she was considered the all-comers bare fist champion of Shrewsbury. Nellie had made considerable sums of money from fighting and was also active in the lucrative smuggling trade that operated on the River Severn between Bristol and Shrewsbury. She could obtain or dispose of any item by means of the river and had been indebted to Doctor Darwin for his advice when channelling her illegal earnings into property. On the Doctor's recommendation Nellie had invested in properties along the river, turning them into lodging houses and this had proved a hugely profitable enterprise, especially at those times when the Severn was either too shallow or swollen to sail. When sailors found themselves unable to continue their journey, Nellie supplied them with female company, which was also the source of a handsome income, with the Doctor providing the girls with medical guidance on cleanliness. Most of the Doctor's involvement with Nellie centred on patching up her facial abrasions as well as those of her two sons, Samson and Hercules, aptly named due to their size and strength.

When Doctor Darwin held parlay with Nellie that morning in the darkened walls of the Elephant and Castle, it took an awful lot for such a credible man to summon up the courage necessary to ask Nellie the ultimate favour.

Her nonchalant reply amounted to little more than, "You just tell me who and consider it done Doctor. Me and my lads will oblige, you've no need to worry."

The Doctor imparted what knowledge he had: the man was called Stanger and had taken a room at The Raven Hotel. Given the wink that Stanger had imparted, Darwin knew he would be seeking the attention of a woman this evening but the Doctor asked Nellie to ensure that after an evening of physical indulgence Stanger was to disappear without trace. All indication of his stay at The Raven must be removed, but as the owner of The Raven took women from Nellie all the time (and wanted it kept a secret), this could be arranged with a minimum of fuss.

Later that night the killer of Hougoumont was laid to rest without military honours in a Shrewsbury cess pool near the Welsh Bridge, which joins the town to Frankwell. This was the site where most of Shrewsbury's toilet waste was emptied. Nobody knew its depth, only the appalling smell it produced and so it was tailor-made for Nellie and her boys' malicious task.

When the disappearance of Stanger was confirmed to him the Doctor felt relief but also a degree of apprehension as he knew others may well follow in Stanger's path of inquiry.

Mattie still remained the weak link of the chain and only drastic measures could keep it intact. Twice now the chain had been tested and managed to survive, but Darwin knew it would not hold indefinitely so decided upon one decisive move to stave off any future probing.

If the episodes with Eyton and then Stanger had caused him consternation, they paled against the anguish he felt at the death of his beloved wife Susannah later that year. They had been childhood friends, lovers and finally a married couple, together for all of their adult lives. He had once confided to a friend, "If anything was to happen to my Susannah, I would never take another woman." With such a large family to look after this was no sweeping statement but his great love and affection for her meant she was completely irreplaceable in his life. Susannah had not been in the best of health for many years of late, which her husband felt was a consequence of the strain childbirth had placed on her small, petite frame and the birth of their last two sons had each proved troublesome as they had both been large babies.

At a party in the Pleasure Garden at the front of Mount House the previous summer, attended by most members of the Wedgwood family, Susannah was heard to say, "Everyone is so young except me." Unnerved by the remark, Darwin recognised it as a sign his wife was giving up her struggle.

Toward the end of her life Susannah had succumbed to invalidity, but during her last few days suffered in great pain with symptoms Darwin recognised as a life threatening condition. He contemplated operating on her with a Chinese herb that brought on a pain-reducing coma but he could not abide the sight of blood and neither did he trust anyone to perform the operation. It was obvious to the Doctor that his wife's appendix had ruptured and with the poison already ravaging her body, was causing constant vomiting and unbearable agony. All through her final illness the Darwin daughters waited on their Mother but all the love and care they bestowed on her could not prevent the inevitable and late on a summer night she died at the age of fifty-two. The following morning, her black dress was laid out on the Doctor's great bed for his wife to be dressed in her coffin, a custom of the times.

The funeral of Susannah Darwin took place at St Chad's Mountford Bridge, on the outskirts of Shrewsbury. The Vicar of the church, a distant relative of the Wedgwood family, was well known to Doctor Darwin and due to a lack of space in the graveyard, Mrs Darwin was buried in the chancel of the church. For the Doctor there followed a period of intense grief, however this time spent mourning his wife was brought to an abrupt end by a matter from the past that refused to remain closed.

SEVENTEEN

The Hero's End

On the evening of Saturday the 3rd of August 1817, Alice Matthews sent word that Mattie required the urgent attention of Doctor Darwin. The Doctor had visited Mattie several times during the past few days and it was evident a rapid deterioration in his health had brought him close to death. As Darwin approached, Mattie made a prolonged choking noise and following one last gurgling sound, the Doctor solemnly announced to those present, "I'm afraid he is gone, God bless him, to a better world than this."

With other formalities already in mind, he stated, "I will arrange the funeral and will be honoured to take Mattie away tonight. I have been attending him all through his convalescence, so I don't see the need for him to be opened up as I have no doubt he succumbed to the grave wounds he received at Waterloo. I dare say it was a miracle he managed to survive so long." The Doctor hung his head in a doleful stance, and breathed an uneasy sigh of unmistakeable relief.

Elsewhere in Shrewsbury that very night, in a public house called The Kings Head a remarkable coincidental twist of fate took place: a soldier that had returned to Shrewsbury after his latest period of active duty began to recount to friends a remarkable tale being told in army circles far and wide, about the reasons behind the outcome of the Battle of Waterloo.

Sergeant Owen from the Cherry Orchard neighbourhood of the town began the story by saying the solider he was about to speak of was the real hero of Waterloo. The assembled group of drinkers took an occasional swig and exchanged astonished glances as Owen furnished them with the following details:

"This one young fellow single-handedly saved the garrison of Hougoumont, no word of a lie! He killed a great French hero, a true giant of a man, by taking off his head with a solitary slash of his sabre! He then went on to hold the French back long enough to close the gate. He took down six Frenchmen before his wounds got the better of him! The maddest part of it all is that in his sick bed that day, he said he wasn't bothered about the garrison, only his horse and a bloody pigeon!"

Owen led the others in laughter and when it had subsided, he continued.

"Oh, it doesn't stop there lads, later that day in one of the squares just beyond Hougoumont, when he was really suffering from his wounds, he saved two wounded cavalry officers! Their horses had been shot from under them. He charged out of the Square just as the French cavalry were trying to cut them down and he fought off the Francs and saved the officers by dragging them back into the square. Men who were there said that after he collapsed again he could not remember any of it due to the massive wound on his head."

The group took a deep, collective breath, swiftly followed by a swig of ale, all in recognition of the man's heroism. If that was a great ripping yarn, Owens's epilogue truly left every man at the table speechless: "This man who I talk of comes from this very town. His home is over the river in Frankwell and he worked for our very own Doctor Darwin from Mount House."

Darwin knew the time had come for loose ends to be tied as best they could. He decided to call the remaining Masons together for a dinner at Mount House where he would inform them of recent developments and of new obligations. As they sat down at the table it became evident that twelve places had been set despite only ten men being in attendance.

"Doctor, are we expecting company?" came an enquiry concerning the two empty chairs around the table.

The room hushed as Darwin began his reply. "The two vacant places are for those who have passed on. The first place belongs to Thomas Eyton, who you all knew." He paused allowing for a moment's reflection, then added: "For those of you who may be concerned, I must tell you that his wife is to be taken care of financially and I trust once again in your silence." Some nodded silently in approval while others seemed unmoved by the disclosure. "The other place is for Mattie, a soldier who carried the pigeon to Waterloo for us, so that I might have the information needed for our financial speculations. He was seriously wounded in the battle and only very recently succumbed to those injuries. His funeral will take place at St Chad's Church on Saturday next. I have been in contact with General Hill who is in the country at the moment and he will bring with him someone to speak of Mattie's heroism at the battle. It will be a big funeral as it is already common knowledge to the people of Shrewsbury that he is a local hero. Therefore I expect a large congregation and turnout so, gentlemen, I am taking this opportunity to tell you that I included Mattie in a financial share for his part in this plot."

With this said, the assembled company rose as one and applauded the fallen hero. When they had finished clapping Doctor Darwin told them, "I would like at this time to thank you for keeping the secret of our deal, which I am sure has earned us all a considerable fortune from our war effort."

EIGHTEEN

The Funeral II
Farewell To A True Hero

The morning of Saturday 23rd August 1817 dawned fine and warm. Doctor Darwin arose early to be informed General Hill and his companions had arrived late in the night. The Doctor was out attending one of his many patients at the time and Edward thought it best not to disturb him, so greetings and introductions were delayed until breakfast.

General Hill had been accompanied to Shropshire by two officers, Colonel Campbell of the Guard's regiment and Lieutenant Colonel Boyle from the Royal Enniskillen Fusiliers, both of whom had served at Waterloo and were fully aware of Mattie's heroics.

General Hill formally introduced the two soldiers to Doctor Darwin. He explained each man knew the brave actions carried out by Mattie Matthews during the battle and were honoured to be speaking at the funeral of a man who had shown such bravery. Over breakfast, talk turned to the peace and prosperity England could now expect due to her victory at Waterloo but when he sensed his guests were sufficiently relaxed, Darwin made a casual enquiry concerning a man named Stanger. The strong reaction of Campbell to the question gave even the Doctor a jolt.

"That murdering bastard! Why we employ people of such a sadistic personality, I do not know. If I had my way he would be on a charge for murder. Do you know he had an insane theory that French sympathisers may have committed treason? He swore he had found evidence that meant this unknown group attempted to bring the country's economy to its knees by selling the currency short? The cockamamie notion was that it came down to a carrier pigeon on the eve of the victory! What utter tripe! The man was clearly beyond help and if the scoundrel turns up again, I hope he's dead!" The line of conversation was dismissed to the sound of "tut, tut" around the table, although Hill and Darwin carefully avoided any eye contact whatsoever. "Anyway," Campbell carried on,

"Wellington, who employed him, has written to the taxation people who he now works for telling them about his torture of French prisoners. He has asked that they drum him out of their service." Quite gratified by what he heard, the Doctor remained silent for the remainder of the breakfast.

The funeral cortege, led by the coffin, slowly made its way to St. Chad's Church. Along the route people stood in silence with heads bowed. When it arrived at the church, the coffin was met by two lines of the town's dignitaries, while a squad of the Enniskillen regiment formed a guard of honour. Behind the coffin followed old Mattie, his wife and family, but there was no sign of Alice who was reported 'too upset to attend'. Inside St Chad's, the coffin, draped in a Union Jack, was placed in front of the altar and when the sun streamed through the stained glass window depicting the Crucifixion, the coffin became shrouded in a pale blue light.

First to address the congregation was General Hill, who apologised for speaking of war on such an occasion but said it had fallen upon him to read out a letter from the Duke of Wellington, commander of British Forces at the Battle of Waterloo. In his letter, Wellington referred to the key elements in his strategy to win the battle, such as the importance of holding the Chateau of Hougoumont on the right flank and the need for the British Square to hold firm. If either had fallen the entire battle would have been lost. The Duke included a personal message of condolence to the loved ones of Private Matthews, "One of many fine Englishman", said the Duke, "who gave their lives for the victory that day at Waterloo." Hill finished speaking and as he did everybody silently stood in homage to the fallen.

Next to speak was Colonel Campbell who introduced himself as the Commanding Officer of the British forces defending Hougoumont. He explained the most crucial time in the struggle to hold the farmhouse came when the French attacked in great numbers at the north gate.

"Initially it looked as if their superior numbers would overrun our defences. Leading a hoard of Francs there was a huge Frenchman standing over six feet tall, a man built like an ox and armed with a great axe. The giant at the front, cheered on by his comrades, made to capture a prize of a horse to take back with him when, from nowhere, a Hussar tore into the giant and with one great chop of his sabre decapitated the Frenchman. This Hussar then cut about him in such away as to send a further six French soldiers to meet their maker. My troops and I on seeing this monumental act of bravery rallied and pushed the French back. We killed nearly all of those that made it through the gate, except for one little drummer boy who we spared."

Among the congregation some listened in awe, others with revulsion, but Campbell proceeded, determined to paint the most graphic picture he could for his captive audience.

"I will say without fear of reprisal that had it not been for this one man, this Mattie Matthews, the chateau of Hougoumont and consequently the Battle of Waterloo would have been lost that day. I visited him later when his wounds were being treated. He was barely conscious and just kept asking about a bird of some sort and how best he could reach the Headquarters. Matthews was in no fit state to leave but later I was told he ignored his wounds with sheer war lust, simply mounting his horse and then re-entered the foray. There is no doubt in my mind that Hussar Matthews was the hero of what happened at Hougoumont that day."

Campbell returned to his seat and was replaced at the pulpit by Lieutenant Colonel Boyle of The Royal Enniskillen Fusiliers. His story continued from where Campbell had roughly finished.

"It was late in the day and the French cavalry were making a great bid to dominate the battle. We were caught in the open and I gave the order for the men to form the square. I noticed a British Hussar make his way into the square on his horse. He was badly injured with wounds bleeding profusely, in spite of many bandages. As he dismounted a shout went up that two cavalry officers on the open ground were about to be run down as both had lost their mounts. Someone grabbed Matthews' horse and made a dash to save them but when he saw this Matthews shot off immediately, shouting at the solider to "dismount and give me back my horse." Boyle looked out at the expressionless faces of the congregation before his thoughts once more returned to events on the battlefield two years previous.

"Matthews rushed out and made straight for the advancing French. When he reached the stranded pair he gave his reins to the one and pulled the other up onto the saddle beside him. He charged back to our square, flaying Frenchies with his sabre as he went.

There was a great cheer from our square and the men started to fight with such renewed vigour that the French withdrew and did not bother the squares again. I went to Matthews to congratulate him but all he kept repeating was "Headquarters" and something about "a bird". He did not make much sense and I humoured him by pointing in the direction of Headquarters, never thinking for a moment that he could or would take off, which he duly did."

After this sardonic comment Boyle risked a slight smile and to his relief found others around the church joined him when he looked to them for approval of the remark. "I found out later that he collapsed at Headquarters and was taken by an adjutant of General Hill to the field hospital. I did not know whether he had survived his ordeal until much later but it is a great honour to be here to tell you that if it were not for Mattie, our square would surely have been broken. God forbid what might have happened then."

As the coffin was taken from the church, Doctor Darwin decided to take a step back and positioned himself, as if hiding, behind one of the great pillars. Watching the congregation file out into the warmth of late morning sunshine, his thoughts turned to the afterlife of a young Hussar no longer with them; the young Hussar, who fourteen hours earlier he had placed on a barge at Mardol Quay for his journey to Bristol, from where he would continue onward to a young land called America.

Mattie and Alice, who had recently discovered she was carrying their first child, could not disguise their bewilderment as they surveyed the Shrewsbury landscape for probably the last time. They stood in silence, eyes fixed upon points in the distance while Darwin explained the necessity and advantage of their sudden departure. He stressed the need of a more agreeable climate to aid Mattie's recovery. The Doctor had given both of them letters of introduction to people of importance in America. People who would find them a splendid home and with investments Doctor Darwin had made on their behalf, they would be wealthy for the rest of their days. Their fortune would grow year on year explained the Doctor, but it was no less than Mattie deserved for the great service he had given to his countrymen. At which point Darwin stopped talking and assisted the young couple as they stepped carefully aboard the barge moored on the quayside. There were hasty, quietly spoken farewells, but within seconds of casting off the barge moved into the shadows cast by the Welsh Bridge and once through the central arch disappeared altogether from view.

Standing alone on the quay, Doctor Darwin watched as the trees on the opposite bank swayed gently from side to side, as if waving Mattie and Alice goodbye. Out on the river a bird dipped and darted inches above the waterline but then turned in flight and headed to the Doctor's side of the river. In the semi darkness he could not tell for sure what breed it was, but soon recognised the unmistakable cooing sound as the bird soared back into the night's sky.

"Impossible," the Doctor had whispered in the isolating darkness. It could never be his beloved Bertie.

Only that morning as he left Mount House, the gardener, Abberly, had called to Doctor Darwin, "Oh Doctor! Your little favourite pigeon Bertie passed on this morning! I told you that many hens being with him might be too much for his little heart. Do want me to throw him on the fire?" The gardener held out the bird's remains, the pigeon's tiny eyes clamped shut and lying still in a small cloth wrap.

"Oh, no" the Doctor had replied. "Bertie deserves a better end than that."

From his vantage point inside the church Doctor Darwin could clearly see across the graveyard and watched as the bearers carried the coffin to its final resting place containing the body of the real hero of Waterloo: A Pigeon called Bertie.

> *"He travelled to a land of enemies,*
> *but died in a land of friends."*

THE END

Printed in Great Britain
by Amazon

34278877R00069